# THE QUEST OF THE
# FISH-DOG SKIN

# BOOKS BY JAMES WILLARD SCHULTZ

My Life as an Indian   1907
With the Indians in the Rockies   1912
Sinopah   1913
Quest of the Fish Dog Skin   1913
On the War Path   1914
Blackfeet Tales of Glacier National Park   1916
Apauk   1916
Gold Cache   1917
Lone Bull's Mistake   1918
Bird Woman   1918
Running Eagle   1919
Rising Wolf   1919
In the Great Apache Forest   1920
Dreadful River Cave   1920
War Trail Fort   1921
Trail of the Spanish Horse   1922
Seizer of Eagles   1922
Danger Trail   1923
Friends of my Life as an Indian   1923
Sahtaki and I   1924
Plumed Snake Medicine   1924
Questers of the Desert   1925
Signposts of Adventure   1926
Sun Woman   1926
William Jackson, Indian Scout   1926
Son of the Navajos   1927
Red Crow's Brother   1927
In Enemy Country   1928
Skull Head the Terrible   1929
Sun God's Children   1930
White Beaver   1930
Alder Gulch Gold   1931
Friends and Foes in the Rockies   1933
Gold Dust   1934
White Buffalo Robe   1936
Stained Gold   1937
Short Bow's Big Medicine   1940

# THE QUEST OF THE FISH-DOG SKIN

## A NOVEL

## JAMES WILLARD SCHULTZ

BEAUFORT BOOKS
Publishers · New York
in association with
Confluence Press

Copyright © 1984 by Museum of the Rockies, Montana State University, Bozeman, Montana

Library of Congress Cataloging in Publication Data

Schultz, James Willard, 1859–1947.
Quest of the fish dog skin.

1. Fox, Thomas, d. 1885?—Fiction. 2. Pitamakan, Siksika chief—Fiction. 3. Siksika Indians—Fiction.
I. Title.
PS3537.C71176Q4 1985     813'.54     83-73495
ISBN 0-8253-0326-5
ISBN 0-8253-0321-4 (pbk.)

Published in the United States by Beaufort Books Publishers, New York, in association with Confluence Press, Lewis-Clark State College, Lewiston, Idaho.

Printed in the U.S.A.     First Beaufort Edition

10  9  8  7  6  5  4  3  2  1

In Memorium

Willard Humphreys
who introduced us
to The James Willard Schultz Society

# THE QUEST OF THE
# FISH-DOG SKIN

## CHAPTER I

It was early in the spring of 1861 that Pitamakan and
I returned to Fort Benton after our perilous winter in the
depths of the Rockies. For a time I was well content to remain within the walls of the stockade and rest and sleep,
and tell over and over to the eagerly listening Company
men the story of our hardships.

A month after our return, however, the factor loaded two
keel-boats and three bateaux with furs and robes, and telling off the crew and putting my Uncle Wesley in charge,
sent them, one fine morning, on their way to far St. Louis.
After their departure I found life in the fort was not so pleasant; I missed my uncle's companionship sorely. True, I went
out with the fort hunter whenever he made a trip for meat,
but as there were now only a few mouths to feed, he hunted
not oftener than once a fortnight, and then for a few hours
only. Why should he? Immense herds of buffalo were constantly grazing in the bottom; in the early morning we shot
them, often from the very walls of the fort.

Moreover, the Blackfeet had all moved out on the far

plains for the summer, and Pitamakan had gone with them; saying that his father needed him to herd the family horses, he had firmly refused to accept our hospitality. Although my uncle's good and faithful wife, Tsistsaki, did all she could to make me happy and contented in our little home, I found the monotony of it all become, week by week, less and less endurable, until at last I actually fell sick from lack of companionship and proper exercise.

If Pitamakan had stayed with me, we could have lounged away the whole summer at the fort—in which event this story would never have been written. It all happened because I was left moping there in the fort, the only boy within its four walls.

Early in August several hundred of the principal Blackfeet came to the fort for a fresh supply of powder and ball, and for two days trade was lively. Their camp, they said, was on the Missouri at the mouth of Sun River. Within a moon they were expecting the River People to join them there for a season of intertribal trade and horse-racing.

Pitamakan's father, White Wolf, was one of the visiting party, and I went quickly up to him to ask about my friend's health.

"Your elder brother sends you greeting," the stern old warrior replied, "and asks you to come and stay with him for a time. There will be great fun for young and old when we and the River People meet."

Without waiting to hear more I ran to Tsistsaki, who was busy at the fireplace preparing her share of a feast for the visitors.

"Pitamakan asks me to go and stay with him!" I cried. "O Tsistsaki! As you love me, let me go!"

# THE QUEST OF THE FISH-DOG SKIN

Rising from the hearth, she gave me a hug and kiss.

"Yes, my son, of course you shall go," she said heartily. "Yes, and I'll go with you. Your uncle will not be here for several moons, so it is right for us to go and live in the great camp for a time. It is long, long since I slept in a lodge. My nostrils are hungry for the odor of trampled sage and the sweet-smelling growth of the plains. My eyes ache for a sight of the happy people as the sun goes down. Yes, my son, we will go to the camp with this party, and have a good time."

So we set out under the protection of Pitamakan's father, White Wolf, who was Tsistsaki's own brother. We each rode a good horse, and we had two pack-animals laden with our bedding, clothing, and food, and with numerous presents for our friends.

I carried a new rifle; that is, it was new for me, although it was a weapon of some age that belonged to my uncle. My own father had made it in the little shop in St. Louis. I took that for a good omen; a sign that I should be fortunate with it. It had a cap lock, and shot a ball weighing thirty-two to the pound. Oh, but I was proud of it, and of the powderhorn and the ball-and-cap pouch slung at my side!

With so good a gun, I did not intend to run short of ammunition; although the kind factor had laughed at me, I had taken, on credit from the Company store, five hundred extra rounds of ammunition and seven boxes of caps, now safely stowed in the centre of one of the packs.

It is about forty miles from Fort Benton to the mouth of Sun River. We left the fort late in the afternoon; not until late in the afternoon of the next day did we draw near

13

to the great camp. It consisted of more than five hundred lodges, scattered in groups on the plain, from the Missouri River for several miles up the smaller stream. The whole valley and the hills on either side were covered with herds of grazing horses, and long before we sighted the camp we could hear the noise of it: the confused, continuous sound of shouting, singing, laughing, drumming, crying of children, the wailing of the bereaved, and the barking of hundreds of dogs.

"Oh, but it sounds good! It sounds good!" Tsistsaki exclaimed.

So it did. As we came nearer and nearer, I knew that I was getting excited. The people saw us coming, and many rode out to greet us. Foremost of them all was Pitamakan, racing across the flat on a big pinto horse. Straight past me he rode with a shout of welcome, wheeled, and coming up beside me, sprang from his horse to mine, just behind the saddle, and gave me a bear-like hug and a kiss. Yes, exactly that, for in those days the embrace and kiss was the Blackfoot salutation among men as well as among women.

"Oh, I am glad to see you again, brother!" my friend exclaimed.

And I answered that I was glad to see him.

"Yonder is our lodge," he said, pointing to one on the right edge of a group of forty or fifty of them; but I had already recognized it by the two enormous otters painted in black and red on the outside, for the otter was White Wolf's sacred medicine-animal.

Pitamakan slid to the ground, caught and remounted his own horse, and presently we halted in front of the lodge.

# THE QUEST OF THE FISH-DOG SKIN

The women, with tears of joy streaming down their cheeks, came hurrying out, and embraced Tsistsaki. They would have kissed me, too, but I managed to elude them under pretense of caring for my horse. They were good old motherly souls, and considered me a real member of the family.

While White Wolf, Pitamakan, and I went inside and sat down on the soft buffalo-robe couches, the women unpacked the horses and brought in the stuff. Then they cooked some buffalo ribs and service-berries for us, a simple meal that we ate with keen appetites.

As the evening advanced, many visitors came and smoked with White Wolf, for they were anxious to hear his news of the fort and its people. There was much talk of the coming of the River People, and of how they should be welcomed to the camp.

I may as well say here that the River People (Ni-é-tuk-tai-tup-î*) were the Indians to whom the early voyageurs gave the name of "Pend d'Oreilles,"—ear pendants,— because they wore such enormous shell earrings. Their home was in the great forests that bordered the big lake and the river that bore their name, and their chief means of subsistence was deer-hunting and salmon-fishing. They also dried immense quantities of camass and bitterroot, articles of food of which the Blackfeet were very fond.

The Blackfeet did not allow the Pend d'Oreilles or the Flatheads, Nez Percés, Kootenais, or any other West-of-the-Rockies tribes, to hunt on their buffalo plains unless they came out of the range to some certain specified point

---

*The vowels are pronounced as in Italian.

15

of meeting. In this instance it had been decided the season
before that the Pend d'Oreilles should come to trade with
the Blackfeet here, at the mouth of Sun River, in the
chokecherry moon—a month that was now at hand. They
were to cross the range by the Sun River Pass, and were
privileged to kill all the buffalo they could on their way to
the meeting-point. That meant much to the people of the
other side; for buffalo meat—best of all flesh—was a
welcome change of diet, and the big, heavy, well-furred
hides answered many purposes for which the skins of deer
and elk were inadequate.

Pitamakan and I passed a pleasant evening, talking over
our experiences of the winter. Early the next morning we
crossed the Missouri at the ford just above the first falls.
Several miles back from the stream I fired the first shot
from my new rifle, and dropped an antelope in its tracks
at a distance of more than two hundred yards. A little later
we each killed a big, fat buck antelope. We now had all
the meat our horses could easily carry, and, although there
were some buffalo farther on, we did not molest them. After
skinning our kills and packing on the meat, we lost no time
in going back to camp. We wanted to be on hand when
the visitors came. Late in the evening some returning
hunters reported that the Pend d'Oreilles were camped on
the Sun River, about a half-day's journey away, and they
would probably trail in on the morrow before noon.

Early the next morning there was a tremendous stir and
bustle of preparation in camp. The women cooked great
quantities of meat,—broiled and boiled,—and got out tempt-
ing portions of rich dried meat, back fat, and bags of berry
pemmican. Then they put on their best buckskin dresses,

16

ornamented with embroidery of beads or colored porcupine quills, and with elk tusks, carefully combed and braided their hair, and painted their faces red or yellow, as their fancy dictated. The men spent much more time on their toilets, and when they had given their beautiful war clothes and eagle-plume war-bonnets a last preening, and had proudly mounted their most fiery horses to ride out to meet the incoming tribe, they were simply gorgeous—a mass of rainbow color.

Pitamakan and I went with them, although in the rear of the chiefs, as befitted our station. Two miles beyond the farther end of the great camp we saw the Pend d'Oreilles coming; their horses raised a trail of dust that mounted into the blue of the mountain sky. There were perhaps a thousand, all told, of the visiting tribe.

The first thing that struck me was that they rode fine big horses of a breed superior to the Spanish stock of the Blackfeet. Then, as they came closer, I saw the men were not physically the equal of the tall, lean, proudly poised Blackfeet. They were shorter and darker. Their hair was in many cases loose and uncombed, and they were not so well dressed. Most of them wore leggings and shirts of buckskin without ornamentation, and togas of the same material. The Blackfeet adopted for their costume whatever was most beautiful in design and color among the different tribes that they met and fought, and in consequence, were the most richly dressed Indians of all the plains.

As we neared the other column, with our chiefs and medicine-men in the lead, we struck up the song of welcome, a powerful chant that quickens the blood. When it ended, the other tribe began its song. We alternated in

17

singing and firing salutes until we met. Then the leaders of both tribes dismounted and embraced one another, sat down, and smoked a pipe of friendship, while we common ones looked on.

"Brother," said our chief, Big Lake, to Ap-o-kai-yo, White Bear, the Pend d'Oreilles chief, "I am glad that you are come into our country, and that we are met this day. In my band of horses is a certain black, swift four-year-old; I give him to you."

"I shall be glad to receive your present," replied White Bear, in fairly good Blackfoot. "I and my children are happy to be with you this day here on your plains. We have looked forward to this day and to meeting you. The gods are good; they have given us a fine day. I take that to be a sign that we shall continue to live in friendship."

There were so many to share in the pipe of peace that it was soon smoked out. When the last whiff had been drawn, the medicine-man, who was master of ceremonies, ostentatiously knocked out the ashes, the party rose and mounted their horses, and the long column proceeded on its way.

Pitamakan and I remained, for a time, where we were, in order to watch the cavalcade. I have never seen a happier lot of men and women and children than the Pend d'Oreilles who filed past us. Their pack-horses, and even some of the horses that they rode, were fairly staggering under the loads of buffalo meat and hides piled on the sacks and panniers of household effects and the stuff that they had brought to trade to us. They were so happy over the success of their short hunt that many of them fairly wriggled in their saddles, and all kept up a constant stream of song and laughter and jokes. Many of the women and children were handsome, but they, like their men, had not such fine clothes as the Blackfeet.

As the column drew near our great camp, each Blackfoot invited one of the Pend d'Oreilles to become his guest, and to set up his lodge close to his own. White Bear camped beside Big Lake, as was natural. Our greatest medicine-man, Red Eagle, had for his guest the head medicine-man of the other tribe, an old fellow named Sees Far. It was this man who was the cause of our great adventure, as I shall relate.

The next afternoon Red Eagle gave a feast to the medicine-men of both tribes. All the morning there had been a lively trade; the visitors swapped fine buckskins, dried camass and bitterroot for our buffalo leather, buffalo-robes, saddles, and trinkets. But all trade was suspended when the time for the feast approached; it was to be in the open air and highly spectacular. During the course of it the Blackfeet Bulls Society were to dance, and every one wished to see them.

Red Eagle's women had cooked a lot of buffalo tongues and ribs, and stewed several kettlefuls of service-berries. At the right time these were brought from the lodge and apportioned to the guests, who sat in a great circle on buffalo-robes spread before a small fire.

After they had eaten and smoked three pipes, the Bulls appeared. Each was a chief. Each wore a mask made of a buffalo bull's head and a toga made of a buffalo-skin, and each carried a bunch of rattles made of dried buffalo dew-claws. Their masks were the complete headskins of bulls, with the horns attached, and so stuffed with hay that

19

they were quite lifelike. The wearers of these stooped far over, so that the masks really rested on the backs of their heads, for otherwise they could not have breathed. They came into the circle dancing slowly, ponderously, to the rhythm of the buffalo song that was sung by the medicine-men. It was a song so weird and solemn that it chilled the heart, and made the little ones weep and hide their faces in their mothers' robes. Round and round the circle danced the Bulls, imitating to the life the stately, heavy tread of the shaggy beasts of the plain; and we, awed by the strangeness of the scene and the harrowing song, sat silent and fascinated. Fear was in our hearts; it seemed as if this were the prelude to some dread catastrophe. I cannot tell how long they danced,—five minutes, ten minutes, perhaps,—but it seemed hours. And then at last the chief Bull led his companions out of the circle, and they danced off behind the near lodges and were gone. The suspense was broken; the people breathed freely once more, and little by little their talk was resumed.

The Pend d'Oreilles medicine-men now gave one of their tribal dances, but after the dance of the Bulls, it seemed tame. It was a pretty dance, however, with a short, quick step. The dance tune or song was sprightly, too, and somehow made me think of the northern lights alternately flashing and dying in the winter sky. The performance did not last long.

Following it, old Sees Far did a dance all by himself that created a sensation. Moving out from the others and seating himself near the fire, he placed in front of him something round and long, inclosed in a painted buckskin sack. For five minutes or more he sat with bowed head, praying, sometimes gently pressing the sack with the palms of both hands, and frequently making the sign for water; by this we knew that his medicine was of the life of the water.

Presently he sang a short song, and untied the mouth of the sack; sang another, and put his right hand into the sack; sang another, and drew out a stuffed skin about three feet long and a foot in diameter, the like of which no one there had ever seen.

It was the skin of a dark-furred animal, with a head like a dog and body without feet or legs. Where the front legs should have been were protuberances that looked like the fins of a fish; behind them the body tapered to a fin-like tail. When the people saw that, their eyes almost popped out of their heads, and with one accord they gave a loud, long-drawn "Ah-h-h!" of surprise.

Four times now, the old man made the sign for water; then, holding the thing out in front of him with both hands, he rose, and, singing a low crooning, quavering song, danced a few steps to the north, then back to the south, then to the east. When he had danced to the west, he stopped, made the sign for water four times again, stooped and picked up the sack and began to draw it over his strange medicine.

"Wait! Wait!" old Red Eagle cried. "Let us see that queer animal." And a hundred voices echoed his request.

Sees Far hesitated, then held up a hand to motion the crowding people back, and said, "Yes, you shall see, but you may not touch it. No, you may not so much as put a finger on it, else my medicine will be broken. Thrice has this medicine-animal saved my life. Twice when I was about to die from sickness, and once when I was waylaid by the

21

enemy."

"What do you call it? Where did it live? Where did you get it?" Red Eagle asked, and we all waited breathlessly for the answer.

"No Pend d'Oreille has ever been where this animal came from," he replied. "I got it from a people whom we call Fish-Eaters, and they got it from a tribe still farther off. A tribe that lives where the big river of the west empties into a salt lake so big that it reaches clear to the jumping-off place of the world. The animal is called fish-dog, because, as they say, it lives only in the water, swimming about like a fish, yet has the face of a dog, and barks like a dog."

"And is it a fierce animal—or fish creature?" someone asked.

"A very dangerous one. Those from whom I got it say that it swims about in large bands, upsets boats, and eats the people when they are spilled into the water."

"Now, that is a medicine-animal!" cried old Stone Arrow, crippled, sickly, yet the richest of all the Blackfeet. "I will give you twenty horses for it! I know it would make me well!"

"No!" said Sees Far, shortly.

"Fifty head!"

"No!"

"A hundred head!"

We all gasped; that was a fabulous price. But again came the answer, "No. Not for all your horses and those of the Blackfeet people will I sell this medicine! I cannot sell it, because it is my life."

Stone Arrow dropped his head, and for a moment was silent. Then, straightening up, he roared, "One of these fish-dog skins I must have! I am sure it would make me

22

well! Whoever will get me one shall choose two hundred head of horses from my band!"

Pitamakan, standing by my side, nudged me in the ribs. "We will go get it for him," he said, confidently.

"Yes, let us go get one for him," I agreed, just as confidently as if the seven or eight hundred miles of perilous traveling that lay between us and the mouth of the Columbia River were but a day's jaunt, and there were no hostile Indians along the trail.

## CHAPTER II

As soon as the feast was over, Pitamakan and I strolled away from the lodges, and sitting down by the edge of the river, began to plan for the quest of the medicine-animal. It was now that my readings in my mother's little library bore fruit. I knew that Sees Far's skin was that of a seal, and that these amphibious creatures lived in the ocean and the tidal waters of large rivers. Also I knew something of geography, and therefore readily understood that the Pend d'Oreille's "big river of the west" was the Columbia River, or, as we called it then, the river Oregon.

"It is very far to the place of the fish-dogs," I said to Pitamakan. "None of the Company men has been there, but I have heard them describe what they have been told about that region. They say that the river is big and swift; so bad in places that a boat would be dashed to pieces. They say, too, that the river is lined all the way by dark forests, and that many tribes of hostile Indians live along its shores."

"What they say is no doubt true. But is it certain that

the fish-dogs live in this river where it joins the big salt lake?"

"Yes, that is sure," I replied. "White men's writings say that where the rivers of the other side empty into the big salt water these animals are plentiful. The skin that we saw just now is proof; it came from the mouth of that big river."

"It is settled, then!" Pitamakan exclaimed. "Come, let's go home and prepare ourselves for the long trail."

We started off swiftly enough, but as we drew near to White Wolf's lodge our steps began to lag; it occurred to us that those in authority would forbid our going on such a dangerous quest.

We found White Wolf sitting alone on his couch at the rear of the lodge. The women were cooking the evening meal of meat and Kootenai tea—leaves of a mountain vine that make a refreshing drink.

We sat down, looked at each other, and fidgeted. Although White Wolf was busy, cutting a pair of leggings for himself from a large side of buffalo cow leather, he occasionally looked across at us, and after a while said:—

"Well, you two, what now? Stop wriggling, and let's hear all about it."

"We want to get a fish-dog for Stone Arrow," Pitamakan replied. "You heard his offer: two hundred horses for a fish-dog's skin."

"Brother, you can do as you please about Pitamakan, of course," Tsistsaki spoke up, "but I say that my boy shall not go on any such hunt. Why, it is said that tribes over there eat people!"

At that my heart sank. For a moment White Wolf was silent: then, as he resumed his work, he said, "Your words are my words, sister. Neither shall my son go into that far and unknown country."

It was Pitamakan's turn to hang his head. Neither of us spoke. Tsistsaki described the dangers to be encountered on such a journey, and White Wolf gave an occasional, "Ah! You speak truth!" in approval of her words. Still we said nothing.

Our portion of the meal was set before us, but as we had no appetite for food, we soon went outside and through the camp again to the river. There we began to express our feelings.

So engrossed were we in talking about what had been said in the lodge, that when a man, walking along the shore, stopped in front of us, we did not look up to see who it was. We were both lying flat on our stomachs, with our heads resting on our crossed arms.

"In this happy time why are you two downhearted?"

We saw Raven looking at us. He was a man of between thirty and thirty-five years; a widower who for two summers had mourned for his wife, and could not be comforted. Since her death he had shunned the gayeties of the camp, and when he was not away on some lone war expedition, he had kept by himself. As a brave and successful warrior, he had great renown.

"We want to go to the big lake of the west and get a fish-dog for Stone Arrow, but they forbid it," Pitamakan said.

Raven sat down beside us. "Tell me about it. What is a fish-dog? Why does Stone Arrow want one?"

After we had told him, he was silent for some time.

"I will go with you," he said, at last. "You shall get a fish-dog skin, and earn the two hundred head of horses."

# THE QUEST OF THE FISH-DOG SKIN

"But they forbid our going!" I exclaimed. "Both Tsistsaki and White Wolf say that we may not go!"

He smiled—a grim, melancholy smile. "Come! We will go to your lodge, and I will talk to them," he said.

Although with little hope that he could gain our point for us, we sprang up and followed him.

If our people were surprised to see him enter the lodge, they did not show it. White Wolf greeted him cordially, gave him the seat of honor on his right hand, and having filled a pipe, passed it to him, while the women were setting out something to eat. Raven ate a little, and then pushed the dish away. When the pipe was lighted again, he began his plea for us.

"We Blackfeet are the richest of all Indians," he said. "We own a larger country than any other tribe, and keep our countless herds of food animals for ourselves. This is because we are brave, trained fighters. You and I, White Wolf, set out to learn the ways of the war trail when we were very young. Our mothers wept at our going, our fathers sat at home with heavy hearts, yet for the good of the whole people they sent us to fight the enemy, and perhaps to die. We are growing old, White Wolf, and others must take our place, else the tribe will perish. Here are two boys, older than we were when we first went to war. It is time they learned the ways of war."

"Oh, no! No, no, no!" Tsistsaki wailed. "Not yet! They are too young! Too young to go to war!"

White Wolf bowed his head, and said nothing.

"The boys tell me that they want to go to the big salt lake of the west, to get the skin of a medicine-animal," Raven continued. "Such a journey would not be a war trail,

27

but it would be good practice for war. Let them go, White Wolf. I will lead the way, and teach them how to pass through the enemies' country, seeing all, but themselves unseen."

"Raven, it shall be as you say." White Wolf straightened up, and looked very fierce. Turning to the women, he said, "Busy yourselves! Prepare the moccasins and the other things necessary for their going."

Tsistsaki, concealing her face in her wrap, began to cry; then, wailing mournfully, she went hurriedly out of the lodge and back from the camp to the sage-brush. We knew that after a while she would return, and without complaining, help to prepare for my journey.

Late the next afternoon a "sweat" lodge was made for us. With Long Bull, the most famous old medicine-man of the tribe, we three went into it. The women passed in hot rocks, and we rolled them into a shallow pit in the centre of the little lodge. They glowed red in the darkness. Dipping a buffalo tail in a dish of water, Long Bull sprinkled them, and then when a dense steam filled the place, prayed long and earnestly for us. The women, listening outside, whimpered, and often exclaimed, "Ai! Kim-is-nat-os. Nó-kos-iks-an-on-kim-is: nuks'uh-ka-mo-ta, nuks'ah-ka-mo-ta." (Yes! Pity them, sun. Our children pity: let them survive, let them survive.)

The old man implored the sun to guard us from all the dangers of the long trail, to give us success in our quest, and to bring us safely back to our kindred.

When the ceremony was over, we wrapped blankets round our dripping bodies, and rushed into the cool and refreshing waters of the river. Then we went home and made preparations for our departure.

The next day there were to be some great horse-races between the Blackfeet and the Pend d'Oreilles. White Wolf urged us to wait and see the races, but although we had been looking forward to the excitement of them, we were now eager only to be off. Raven came from his brother's lodge, and called us; Tsistsaki, crying silently, kissed me and hugged me; Pitamakan's mother embraced him; we picked up our belongings, and went out. White Wolf followed. Raising his hands to the sky, he cried:—

"O sun! O you sacred ones of the above, and the earth, and the deep waters: have pity on these, my children, and bring them safely back to me!"

Without another word on either side, we turned our backs on the lodge, walked through the great camp, and struck up the valley toward the mountains.

Our outfit for the long trail was simple. In order to save the powder and balls for their flintlock, smoothbore guns, Pitamakan and Raven carried bows and quivers of arrows. Besides a filled horn and a ball pouch, I carried two bladders full of powder, a sack of two hundred balls, and caps to match. We each had a sheath-knife, flint, and steel, a half-dozen pairs of moccasins, and an awl and some sinew thread for mending our moccasins and our clothing. I wore woolen trousers, a woolen shirt, and a fustian capote; but I knew that somewhere along the trail I would have to do some tanning, and dress in buckskins, as the others did. We each had a thick, four-point blanket slung on our backs; in it were rolled our small belongings and our store of footwear.

Keeping on the east side of the river, and traveling at

a good pace all day, we came at evening to the foothills of the great mountains. At the mouth of the river gorge I shot a white-tail deer. We built a fire, roasted some of the meat, and ate it with keen appetite. After the sun had gone down, we went on for a mile or more, and finally lay down in a thick grove of willows.

"Butterfly, give me good dreams. Above People, have pity on us; give us full life," Raven prayed, as he wrapped his blanket round him and stretched himself on the soft ground.

"The night is my happy time," he said to us. "Not always, but often when I sleep, my shadow goes forth, and I meet her. Always she is the same; kind and gentle and loving. At first I felt that I must go, too; but one night my shadow went forth and met hers, and she said, 'Keep on living; the people need you; do good to all; I shall be proud of the great name you will have.' So, my young brothers, I stay and do what I can for her sake, but the time is long; the time is long."

Lying beside him, I felt that he shivered. As neither Pitamakan nor I knew what to say to him, we were silent.

At the first sign of dawn, we made up our bundles and went on, carrying, to eat by the way, some of the deer ribs that had been roasted the night before. On Sun River, not far back in the mountains, there is a tremendous cañon; of its rugged and gloomy depths we had many glimpses from the trail that ran beside it. First the hordes of game, then the mountain Indians had worked out this path round the impassable bed of the river.

The Pend d'Oreilles had but recently traversed it; the prints of their horses' feet were still fresh in the dust. So plentiful at this time was the game that the passing of hundreds of hunters had left no apparent effect upon its numbers.

On every side we saw herds of deer and of elk, and small groups of buffalo—mostly bulls. Occasionally a moose trotted swiftly out of our way into the brush. Bands of sharp-eyed bighorn watched us uneasily from the tops of near-by buttes, and more than once during the morning we circled out from the trail, in order to avoid a possible encounter with grizzly bears. Singly, and by twos and threes,—once in a band of seven,—they shambled along the mountainside, sniffing, overturning stones, and tearing rotten logs apart in search of insects. Once we came suddenly upon an old male that was stripping the half-ripe fruit from a chokecherry bush. Hearing the soft shuffle of our moccasined feet, he whirled round, sat up on his haunches, his enormous forepaws drooping, and looked directly at us with his wicked, smoke-colored, pig-like eyes.

As the wind was from him to us, he could not get our scent, and thus we stood for what seemed an interminable time of suspense. If he decided to charge, one of us would get hurt, perhaps killed, before we could kill him. Our two flintlock guns were not good weapons with which to meet grizzlies.

Presently the old fellow expelled his breath in a faint "Woof!" He snorted louder and louder, and finally, with a last explosion, he got down on his feet and moved away from us sidewise into a more distant patch of brush. He had not made out what we were, and the unknown had its terrors for him.

At the upper end of the cañon we looked down on a wide and beautiful grassy valley, dotted with groves of pine and quaking-asp. Like a silver serpent the cottonwood-fringed river wound through it. To the west of the valley rose the rough peaks of the divide; on the east was the chain of smaller mountains bordering the plains.

Pointing to a depression in the side of the valley, several miles away, Raven said:—

"In that place is a spring of hot, bad-smelling, bad-tasting water that is great medicine. It has wonderful power; the ill, by bathing in it, are made well. The well come out of it refreshed and stronger than ever."

"Let us go bathe in it," said Pitamakan, and I echoed his words.

But that was not to be.

"Look!" exclaimed Raven. "See what is there! There, coming along the trail this side of the spring!"

Even as he started to speak our eyes had also made the discovery. From a grove of pines, a long way off, several men on foot were coming along the trail. As they were in single file and close one behind another, we could not count them; we guessed their number to be between thirty and forty.

"A war party!" Pitamakan exclaimed.

"Yes, and following the trail of the River People, to raid their herds and those of the Blackfeet," said Raven.

"In some way we must turn them back," he added, in a moment; "we must think quickly how to do it."

I proposed that we turn back ourselves, go straight home with all possible speed, and warn the people of the enemy's approach; but Raven would not listen to that.

"It is bad luck to turn back after starting on such a trail as this," he said. Pitamakan agreed with him that it was not to be thought of.

We were standing under some scattered pines at the rim of the hill, and the war party had not discovered us. Soon, when they had entered another grove, we moved up to the right of the trail into a dense thicket where we knew we could not be seen. But there were our footprints plain in the dusty path, the *parflèche* soles of our moccasins betraying the fact that not mountain people but Blackfeet had recently passed. If the war party should come to the telltale signs, they would scatter and hunt us; and what were three against forty?

We saw the enemy come out of the little grove and swing along toward us at a lively gait. As the minutes passed, Pitamakan and I anxiously waited for Raven to speak. He stood in deep thought, apparently neither seeing nor heeding anything about us. We grew more and more anxious. At last I could stand the suspense no longer.

"Tell us what we are to do!" I pleaded, touching his arm. "Can't you see how fast they come?"

He straightened up like a man roused from sleep, and I suspected that, even in face of the enemy, his thoughts had been of his lost wife.

"The one way to turn them back is to let them know that we are Blackfeet, and to make them think that we are a large party," he answered, calmly, almost listlessly.

"Ah!" Pitamakan and I exclaimed, and waited breathlessly for him to explain.

"You boys stand right here," he said. "I will go along the side of the valley until I get opposite them—keeping in the brush all the time, and out of their sight. When I begin to shoot at the party as fast as I can and shout the Blackfoot war cry, you do the same, standing right here until you have fired and reloaded three or four times from that clump of pines; then hurry down below the trail, and shoot from the timber, and remember to give the war cry while shooting, clapping your mouth with your hands and changing your voice often so that they will think you are a large party.

"And now, listen! Look sharp! You see that second mountain there to the west, the one with the round summit lifting above the timber? Well the top of that will be our meeting-place. If we become separated, make for that as soon as you safely can. If I am not there, wait for me a day and a night; then if I don't come, you will know that I am dead, and you must make your way home as best you can, and tell the people that Raven has gone to the Sand Hills to join his wife. Now, do you understand all that I have said?"

We replied that we did and without another word he left us. Twenty or thirty yards away the brush swallowed him, and we saw him no more.

Inaction in the face of great danger is the most trying thing in the world. Our natural inclination was to turn and run, and to keep on running and walking until we should be safe at home. But that was not to be considered for a moment. Instead, we were put to the test of warriors: to follow exactly the orders of our chief. But the waiting was cruel; the uncertainty about the outcome of it all was harrowing.

Although time dragged, the war party came all too swiftly down the trail. When they were a mile away, we thought that Raven should open fire. When they were less than a half-mile distant, we began to think that in some way he had failed us. On they came, without once stopping. At last we could count them: thirty-seven in all. Gun-barrels gleamed in the sun; at least a third of the party, however, walked with both hands swinging free, and this showed that they were armed only with bow and arrows, slung in the quiver at their backs.

They approached the lower end of the valley, less than a quarter of a mile away.

"We can't wait much longer," Pitamakan said.

But we did wait, and if our faces expressed what we felt, they must have appeared wild-eyed from fright.

At last the party began to climb the steep ridge on which we stood, and through which the river had cut its deep-walled way. Just as they came over the first rise, and stood for a moment to regain their breath, Raven's gun sounded off to their right. Following the report, we heard the Blackfoot war cry.

Then we fired our pieces, elevating them many degrees, in hope that the balls might do some damage. After Raven's shot, the party turned and faced in the direction from which it had come. But when we fired and raised our quavering yells, they scattered in all directions, like a brood of grouse fledglings, and disappeared as quickly. I could hardly believe my eyes. Some ran down the hill and over to the cotton-woods fringing the river; others ran toward us into berry-bush thickets and stands of tall rye-grass; still others scattered into a growth of young pines in Raven's direction. Obeying our orders, we continued to load and fire, shout the war cry, and aim at the places in which the enemy lay concealed; they answered with never a shot or a shout.

We rushed up the hill, and fired a few times from the

pines; then we ran down below the trail, and shot from the dense thicket, in each place shouting the war cry in high key and low key, with hoarse and clear voice. And then we realized that Raven had stopped shooting. We ceased, too, and not a sound was to be heard anywhere except the raucous calling of a Clark's crow.

"Now what?" I asked Pitamakan. "What shall we do now?"

"I don't know. Let's stand here for a time, and watch and think," he replied.

Soon we began to catch glimpses of moving forms, merely the top of a black head or the outline of a bent back. In one place a bunch of rye-grass swayed sharply; in another, the bushes of a thicket trembled; the enemy, with the intention of surrounding and entrapping us, were spreading out. Our shooting and shouting had been worse than useless; we had not driven them back; instead, we now had to fall back.

Motioning me to follow him, Pitamakan started obliquely back across the hill toward the cañon.

"Don't go there," I said. "Let's run along the trail nearly to the plains, then turn and circle this way."

Pitamakan did not approve of this suggestion; he did not answer except by a shake of the head. Then he broke into a run, and there was nothing for me to do but follow.

# CHAPTER III

After running about two hundred yards, we came to the place where the mountain broke down into the cañon. There was a very steep slope of thirty or forty yards, beyond which we could see nothing but the jagged black and red wall on the far side of the tremendous chasm. The slope was grassy and slippery, but here and there stood a few small pines, and Pitamakan ran down from one to another of them, bringing up at each one with a jerk that threatened to wrench his arm off. I hesitated to follow, but he called me sharply, and I was soon with him, hanging to a tree at the lower edge of the slope.

From there an almost perpendicular wall of rough and creviced rock extended down for about ten feet to a narrow shelf that was the top of the great cliff of the cañon. At the point where we stood, it was possible to descend this wall by way of a rough V-shaped crack, but so far as we could see in either direction, there was no other escape. To our left the shelf narrowed rapidly and ran out; to the right it curved under a huge, over-hanging rock.

"We will climb down to that shelf, and go along it to the bend, where the wall sticks far out over it," said Pitamakan. "There we shall be safe enough. No one can see us from the top, or from any other direction."

He started down the crevice, then stopped and looked back up the slope. "Oh, see what you have done!" he cried. "That betrays us."

He pointed at a gash in the grassy slope; the sod and black earth were torn away in a narrow strip. Without thinking of the mark it would leave, I had come down in a sitting position, holding my rifle between my legs and pressing the sharp butt plate into the soft ground to check my momentum. I felt so chagrined that I could not look at my friend.

"Well, it is done now, and can't be undone." he said. "Perhaps they will not notice it. Come on, let's get down at once."

The descent of the crevice to the shelf was not difficult. We soon made it, and keeping close to the wall, walked along the narrow way to the bend. At that point a layer of soft sandstone under the hard cap-rock had worn away, and had made the shelf fully ten feet wide. We went far enough to be sure that our position was unassailable from any place beyond, then came back to a point from which we could watch the crevice. There we broke off some bushes, arranged them naturally on the shelf for a screen, and lay down.

"Do you think that they will find the rip in the slope, and try to get down?" I asked.

"They may, but look! Only one man, gripping the rock with both hands, can come down that crevice at a time,"

Pitamakan replied. "We can kill them as fast as they appear."

We thrust our rifles through the leafy screen, cocked the hammers, lay perfectly still, and listened for any sound above. From far below, the muffled roar of the river came up to us; with outspread wings an eagle circled close overhead; in a crack in the rock a chipmunk dug for roots. It was hard to believe that in that wild and remote spot men were searching for us to take our lives.

All at once, after we had lain there for more than an hour, Pitamakan signed to me that he heard something above. A few small stones rattled down the crevice upon the shelf. These were soon followed by heavier pieces loudly clattering, and then came into view part of a man's body clad in dingy buckskin. The crevice concealed his legs and waist, and part of his back, but as he made his way cautiously down, more and more was revealed, until his shoulders and head were in plain sight. When we saw his face, we both gave an involuntary start. He was the leader of the Kootenai band that at the beginning of the winter before had stripped us of all our belongings.

"I'll shoot," Pitamakan whispered. An instant later, with a click and a sputtering of the powder in the pan, his old flintlock boomed.

What followed the report I saw only dimly through the smoke. Without a cry, the man pitched head first down the crevice, struck the narrow shelf on his back, and bounded off into space. We heard the startled cries of his companions. I shuddered; but Pitamakan said calmly, "It

---

*See *With the Indians in the Rockies*

is a pleasant task to kill one's enemies. He will never rob us again."

All was now as quiet as before. Pitamakan reloaded, and we lay behind our screen, listening, and wondering if any more of the enemy would try to come down the crevice. After a few minutes, we heard a faint shot, followed by several others, apparently from a long distance east; and we concluded that Raven was trying to draw the enemy away from us.

"Some of them will follow him, and some will stay up there at the top of the slope," Pitamakan said. "They think that we must either die of thirst or die fighting them."

"And so we must. When we started down the slope, I thought that we were going into a trap!" I exclaimed.

"We are not trapped yet," he said. "When we came to the rim of the cañon, I saw a bighorn go down into the crevice; there is some kind of a trail running below from here. Besides, I counted on Raven; he will not let us perish here. If he sees that the enemy have us cornered, he will save us if he has to get help from the camp to do it."

"But suppose he is killed, and there is no trail going down from here?" I suggested.

"Brother, my medicine is very strong," Pitamakan said, impressively. "It is something that I can't explain, but this I know: it made me run toward the cañon, it urged me down the slope, and to this place. Why, I could almost hear it telling me what to do; I surely felt it pushing me this way. So do not worry; we shall survive."

But I did worry. It seemed as if the hot afternoon sun would never go down; the far-off roar of cool water became almost maddening. How I craved a long, deep draft of it!

# THE QUEST OF THE FISH-DOG SKIN

When the sun dropped behind the western peaks, Pitamakan told me to watch the crevice, and then little by little he edged back from the screen, turned round, and crept away along the shelf. When he at last came back, I could see by his grin that he had good news.

"There is a trail," he said. "Not far beyond the bend this shelf dips down to another that is directly under us, and that runs into a big, rough break in the lower part of the cliff. I have proof that it is a trail. There are bighorn tracks in some earth that has freshly fallen upon the shelf, and the animals that made them have disappeared."

He explained that although there was one place on our shelf, a space of fifteen or twenty steps, where we could be seen by persons on top of the wall, no one would be watching there. The enemy, believing that the only way for us to get out was by climbing the crevice, would guard that and no other point.

That seemed plausible. We decided to try to escape by the trail as soon as there was enough light from the moon. The moon was full, but it would be midnight before it rose high enough to light up the walls of the cañon.

Early in the evening we heard the enemy talking on the slope above. Once we were startled by a rattling of pebbles in the crevice; it was then so dark that we could see nothing beyond the screen. We reasoned, however, that any one actually coming down would start the larger rocks clattering; and later the increasing light of the moon revealed our shelf bare of any suspicious-looking object.

When the moon was near the zenith, but while the shelf was still in dark shadow, we started. We went forward with slow, careful steps, and kept close to the wall. Pitamakan nudged me and pointed upward when we came to the place where the overhanging cap-rock had broken off, and allowed the moonlight to stream down upon us. It was with sickening apprehension that we stole along there, not daring to look up lest we should lose our footing. Upon passing again into shadow, we were so unnerved that we were obliged to stop and rest.

The shelf descended at a steep angle to the next one. At the junction we turned and went in the opposite direction. For the first part of the way this shelf was about fifteen feet wide, but after a time it narrowed rapidly, and at last Pitamakan halted, and exclaimed, "We have come to the end of it!" After a moment, he added, "No, we haven't. I believe that there are some footholds, but I can't see them plainly; we must wait here for more light."

Except for the dim, reflected light from the opposite wall, our side of the cañon was still dark. We spent an anxious hour waiting. At last the moon passed the meridian and lighted up the rocks all round us; for a distance of fifteen or twenty feet the width of the shelf varied from two inches to eight or ten inches, and in places there was nothing except the wall of the cañon, dropping straight down for thousands of feet. Again and again we measured the blank spaces with our eyes; none seemed so wide that we could not step across it, and all along above, there were projections and cracks that would afford finger-holds.

As we had to have both hands free in order to make the passage, we fastened our rifles to the packs. Pitamakan cautioned me to pull or twist everything I took hold of to make sure that it was solid. We started. Most of the way, with our faces pressed against the rock, we fairly hugged the cliff. In one place, where a very wide step had to be made, I lost my balance, and but for Pitamakan would have toppled off into the awful chasm; just in time he caught my hand, and with a quick pull, helped me to reach his side!

The passage of that dangerous place was an experience that I shall never forget. The horror of it remained with us after we regained the broad and solid shelf. We came soon to what Pitamakan had called a break in the lower part of the cliff; it was more than that; from above he had not been able to see that it was a deep fissure worn by water. In one direction, it led back into the mountain; in the other, it ran down to the river. We worked our way to the bottom of it, and then stood undecided which way to turn. At that point the bed was sandy, and running up and down it was a well-worn bighorn trail.

"If we go down into the big cañon, we may find no way to get out," said Pitamakan.

"If we go up it, we may run right into the enemy," I answered.

"Well, let us take that chance!" he exclaimed. "At any rate, up there on top of the mountain there is room to run!"

We went up, and at the end of the sand-bed found a pool of water in a hollow of the bed-rock. It was what we craved above all things. We drank and drank, and then went on with renewed strength and courage.

In places the way was over immense boulders; farther up there was a series of little cliffs, and afterward steep, smooth chutes, where several times we lost our holds and went sliding back. But at last we came to the end of the fissure, and found ourselves in a grove of pines on the top of the mountain, and fully a half-mile from the place where, no doubt, the enemy were still lying in wait for us. We agreed that there was little chance that any of them were near us; nevertheless, we stole cautiously back from the cañon for more than a mile, and jumped the Pend d'Oreille trail when we came to it, in order to leave no telltale footprints.

"We must let Raven know that we have escaped," said Pitamakan.

"It can't be done," I answered. "We must make our way to the meeting-place mountain and wait for him to join us there."

"But there is a way to let him know where we are," Pitamakan said. "Your rifle makes a sharp, quick report, very different from the long, heavy boom of our flintlock smoothbores. We will shoot, one after the other, then run toward the plains, and shoot again, and then circle round into the valley and go up to the meeting-point. If Raven hears the shots, he will say, 'Ah, they have escaped from the cañon! The enemy does not answer the shots; the boys are not pursued; they are telling me to meet them on the mountain.'"

It took a long time to carry out this plan. After firing the last round, we circled down into the valley and crossed the river on a shallow ford. Day began to break when we left the stream and climbed up through the heavy pine forest toward the meeting-place. Late in the morning, completely worn out, we arrived at the top of the mountain; within two minutes we were both sound asleep.

"Man-i-kap-iks, kak-it-so-yit!" (Young men, come and eat!)

The words half-awoke me, and I thought them a part of a dream until they were repeated. Then I roused myself,

44

to find Raven by our side. "Come on," he said. "I have made a kill and we will feast."

We sprang up, slung on our packs, and followed him down the mountain into a deep ravine, where lay a big bull elk he had killed with his bow. We quickly gathered some dry sticks that would burn without giving off enough smoke to reach above the treetops. With his flint and steel, Pitamakan started a fire.

While we waited for the meat to be cooked, Pitamakan told the tale of our adventures, and Raven briefly related his experience. When he had learned of his failure to draw all of the enemy after him, and had realized that we were under siege in the cañon, he had crept up as close as he dared, only to hear us shooting away off on the mountain. Then, hoping to get a shot at the enemy as they followed our shots, he had hurried back to the trail, but had seen nothing more of the band.

After daybreak he had made a wide circle, had found their tracks in the trail in the valley, and had followed them far enough to make sure that the enemy were heading back toward their country. He had concluded that our shooting convinced them that we had escaped from the cañon, and that we would come back with a big party.

After a hearty meal, we took as much of the elk meat as we could carry, and moved up to the hot medicine-spring. There we remained two days, in order to give the enemy a long start of us. About half of that time we spent bathing in the spring. I did not then know that sulphur caused the disagreeable odor and taste of the water.

Early in the morning of the third day we took the trail again. It went straight up to the head of the wide valley, then turned due west up the great divide between two lofty mountains. The sun was setting when we came to the summit and looked out on the other slope, a dark green forest apparently without end, broken here and there by small ranges of gray mountains. To us of the open plains, there was something sinister about that outlook, and so deeply did it impress us that Pitamakan and I, inveterate chatterboxes, were silent.

Raven almost never spoke from one day's end to another, except to give orders, or instruct us in the ways of the war trail, but I could see that even he was oppressed, and I caught some of the words of the short prayer he muttered: "O Above People! You, O Sun, and you his wife, O Nightlight! And you, Morning Star, their powerful son! Preserve us from the evil spirits of these dark woods. Save us from the peoples of this side, and from all the dangers of the trail. Help us to do that which we have set out to do, and to return to our own buffalo plains."

"Kyi! Night comes on," said Raven, after a pause, and he led the way down the slope.

A mile below the summit we turned from the trail into a dark ravine, ate sparingly of our small store of cooked elk meat, drank deeply from a Pacific streamlet, and lay down. It was soon evident that we had camped in the midst of immense herds of elk. All round us the bulls were whistling, charging wildly through the timber, and clashing antlers against antlers in furious combat. Not far below us, some yelping timber-wolves attacked a band of elk. We heard the great animals crash away through the timber in all directions. For a few moments one bleated pitifully; then the pack growled and yelped, as they tore the quarry's flesh.

# THE QUEST OF THE FISH-DOG SKIN

Whereupon Pitamakan softly hummed the wolf-song, which was believed to bring good luck to hunters, and to war parties penetrating the country of the enemy. So great was the uproar of the forest creatures that, tired as we were, it was long before we slept.

At daybreak Raven went a short distance up the ravine and shot a fat white-tail buck with his bow. We spent half the morning roasting a quantity of the meat to take with us; in the country of enemies, the fewer fires we built the better.

Until late in the afternoon our course was downhill. Then we climbed the side of a small mountain range; from the top we had a glimpse of the far-away waters of Flathead Lake. We stopped for the night on the top of the range, and while we ate our cold roast meat, Raven made plans for the next day.

He said that the Flatheads were undoubtedly camped at the foot of the lake, or near it, and that, although the Blackfeet had met them in friendship the summer before, they were an uncertain people, and we had better avoid them. In order to do that, we should have to leave the trail upon reaching the foot of the range and travel parallel with it, stop if we sighted a camp, and wait for night before passing round it. We little knew what was really to happen!

About the middle of the next afternoon we emerged from the heavy forest and found ourselves on the edge of a wide and beautiful plain that was dotted with small groves of pine and cottonwood. The nearest of these was fully a mile away, and for a time Raven was undecided whether we had better go on to it, or wait where we were until night. Pitamakan was in favor of going on, and finally he had his

47

way.

But before we had traveled a quarter of the distance, out from the forest to the right of where we had emerged came forty or fifty riders, driving and leading heavily laden pack-animals, and at once four or five men charged toward us. When they saw that we were strangers, they made the peace sign.

"They are Flatheads," Pitamakan said. "I know their faces. All is well."

The recognition was mutual. The Flatheads knew my companions, and dismounting, embraced each of them. None of the Flatheads could speak Blackfoot, but by signs the leader told us that the big camp of his people was not far away, and that we were to go there to rest and feast. He made it plain that all the people would welcome us and treat us well.

We accepted the invitation—without giving offense there was nothing else we could do. The band had been on an elk hunt, and was returning with all the meat and hides that the horses could stagger under. It was dusk when we came to the big camp near the foot of the lake, and as was proper, the leader of the band escorted us to the lodge of the head chief, who stood just outside the doorway to make us welcome. The fire had been allowed to die down within, and we could hardly see the places pointed out for us on the right side of the lodge. On the opposite side several persons were sitting. The chief gave an order to his women, and one of them placed some wood on the fire. Presently the flame leaped up, and all was made plain as day.

Pitamakan and I started as if we had been shot. Menacingly staring at us across the fire were two Kootenais, whom we recognized as belonging to the party that had taken our belongings from us in the Rockies the winter before. One of them had a bandage round his right arm, and he, glaring evilly at Raven, whispered to his companion; then they both smiled in a gloating way.

The Flathead chief noticed this, and seemed uneasy. He started to speak, but just then the door curtain was thrust aside, and in came four more Kootenais. Evidently the whole party that we had driven back were in the camp and we were in a desperate situation.

# CHAPTER IV

The newcomers took seats beside their two comrades.
The Flathead chief lighted and passed a pipe to Raven; he
took a few whiffs of smoke, and passed it back. The chief
then offered it to the Kootenai nearest him, the one with
a broken arm; but he refused it with an indignant gesture,
and began to talk excitedly, pointing at Raven and then
at his arm, and again at Pitamakan and me.

We could not understand a word of the language, but
it was plain that he told of the conflict between us on the
other side of the mountains. When he stopped talking, the
other Kootenais had their say in turn, each one glaring
angrily at us as he spoke.

The Flathead did not reply to them, but listened with
bowed head, and mechanically rubbed his long, smooth
pipestem. When the last one of them finished talking, the
Flathead spoke a few words to one of his women, and she
went out of the lodge. In a few moments she returned
accompanied by a fine-looking young man, whom my companions greeted in Blackfoot. He took his seat on my left.

50

Pitamakan leaned over and whispered to me:—

"He is Young Otter, the half-blood; his mother is a Blackfoot."

The Flathead chief talked for some time to Young Otter, who then turned to us and said, "These Kootenais accuse you of attacking them in the valley of Sun River, of killing one of their party, and wounding that man sitting there."

"They speak the truth," Raven answered. "I broke that one's arm."

"When I fired," said Pitamakan, proudly, "the man tumbled from the cliff and dropped to the bottom of the big cañon."

Young Otter interpreted these answers, and immediately all the Kootenais excitedly harangued the chief. He listened to them patiently; when they were done, the interpreter told us that they demanded our lives in payment for their loss.

"Say this to your chief for me," Raven calmly answered. "The other side of the backbone-of-the-world is the Blackfoot country. They were invading it for the purpose of stealing our horses. We did to them only what it was our duty to do."

As Young Otter repeated this, Pitamakan whispered to me, "The Kootenais and Flatheads have always been friends and allies; keep your rifle ready for use. If they get their way, we will kill the three nearest the chief right here, and as many more as we can before we die."

Then he turned to Raven and repeated what he had said to me. Raven nodded. The outlook for us seemed dark, indeed. I must have shown by the expression of my face how I felt, for Young Otter nudged me and whispered, "I-ká-ki-mat!" (Take courage!)

# THE QUEST OF THE FISH-DOG SKIN

Breathlessly I waited for the old chief to speak. Now and then one and another of the Kootenais addressed a few words to him, and still he kept his head down, and twirled and smoothed the pipestem with his long, lean, delicate hands. I cannot describe the suspense of these moments; but I know how an innocent man accused of murder feels as he waits for the jury to decide his fate.

The Kootenais became more and more importunate, until all were again talking at once. At that the old man lifted his hand to command silence, and addressed them in their own language.

Young Otter interpreted it for us. "One summer ago, in the moon of ripe cherries, we Flatheads smoked and made peace with the Blackfeet. We are few in number because of wars with them in the past. On our part, we shall do all in our power to keep this new-made peace. I cannot give the white boy and two Blackfeet into your hands. You must not harm them while they remain in my village. What happens to them or to you after they leave here is none of my concern. They came to visit us, I believe. Well, they shall remain as long as they please, and go when they please."

The Kootenais began to expostulate almost before the old chief finished speaking. That made him angry, and straightening up in his seat, he pointed a finger at them and shouted, as we were told later:—

"Shut your mouths! I have said! So it shall be!"

In the faces of the Kootenais came a stony, set look that it was not pleasant to see. A large crowd of men had collected outside to hear what was being said in the lodge, and when their chief angrily refused the Kootenais' demand, most of them, as we could tell by the tone of their voices, expressed their approval.

Within, Young Otter was the next man to speak. Leaning forward in his seat and looking at the Kootenais, he said to them, "My father is the war chief of this tribe. As he is away now, my words are his words. You may intend to shoot these guests of ours as they pass to and fro in the camp, or as they sit round the evening fire in our lodges. Think well before you do this; for everyone of them you kill, it will be our unpleasant task to take a Kootenai life. I have said."

Our enemies did not reply to this. Young Otter then spoke to the chief, who emphatically showed his approval; whereupon the young man invited us to be his guests. Gladly we followed him out through the crowd and to a fine, big lodge on the other side of the camp, where his mother received us as if we were her own sons.

Seldom have I heard a woman talk faster or ask more questions than this good Blackfoot mother did. Moreover, she could do several things at once; while she was asking about the welfare of her relatives and friends, and alternately laughing and crying, according to the news we gave of them, she was boiling, broiling, and stewing food. Soon she set before us heaping wooden platters of meat, camass root, bitterroot, stewed service-berries, and, rarest treat of all, small lumps of bitter-sweet sugar, made by boiling the sap of soft maple trees. It was far better fare than we had at the fort.

For a time, the good meal and the lively talk of our hostess diverted our thoughts; Young Otter reminded us of the seriousness of our position by telling his mother to cover the fire with ashes. "We can talk in the dark just as well," he added.

We all agreed that, although there would be no risk in our wandering about the camp in the daytime, the Kootenais might try to shoot us by aiming at our shadows cast by the fire on the lodge skin. Young Otter said that he was sure the enemy would watch us day and night, and if we left the camp, would follow close on our heels. He advised us to remain with him indefinitely, and trust to some lucky chance to escape from their vigilance. Raven pronounced this the only thing to do. So we lay down, with guns by our side, and slept fitfully until sunrise.

I was surprised to find the Flatheads a most kindly and hospitable people. During the days that we remained with them we were invited to their feasts and to dances of different kinds, and given seats of honor, much to the disgust and anger of the Kootenais, one or more of whom followed wherever we went. I must say here that in those days the Flatheads were a clean and moral people, affectionate to their children, and eager to do everything they could to make happy the lot of the old people. They were a good-looking race; most of them were tall, muscularly slender, and of fine features, and many of the women were really beautiful.

The camp was pitched at the extreme southern end of the lake, which is fully thirty miles wide. Sometimes a strong northwest wind raised a heavy sea, a novel sight to Pitamakan and me, and we spent much time watching the big green rollers break upon the shore. One day, while we were thus occupied, a thought came to me which my companions afterward declared must have been inspired by the gods; they declared that I was great medicine.

# THE QUEST OF THE FISH-DOG SKIN

"If we had a boat," I said, "we could paddle away from here some evening, paddle away into the darkness, and escape from the Kootenais."

"True! True!" Pitamakan exclaimed. "But there is no boat, not one on this big water."

"There shall be one!" I cried, springing up. "Come on! Come quick with me to the lodge!"

We burst in upon our hosts so suddenly that Young Otter dropped his pipe—a bad omen—and his mother shrieked. I excitedly unfolded my plan; that they should make a skin boat for us, like those I had often seen built by the Company men at the fort. I told them that I would make a small model for them to copy on a large scale, about five paces long.

I explained that they could build the frame-work in the thick woods near the shore, while we in the lodge sewed together enough elkskins to cover the frame. Then, some still evening after they had stretched the covering on the frame, had allowed it to dry, and had pitched the seams, they could tow the boat to the camp, and we could paddle away in the night to a place where the Kootenais could not find us.

As Young Otter thought this a fine plan, I went to work at once, and made a frame model about a foot long. His mother, taking the skins she had, and borrowing from friends the others that we needed, put fourteen elkskins to soak in the lake. It was no small task to cut those skins and sew them together in an oblong sheet that tapered toward each end from the centre, but Pitamakan and I accomplished it in four days, although our fingers were worn raw by the sinew thread. In less time than that Young Otter and his mother made the boat frame; the gunwales were of two strong green fir poles and the ribs of young birch, all bent to shape and fastened with rawhide wrappings. Then while they collected spruce-gum for pitching the seams, put on the skin and sewed it in place, we made two paddles. In about a week from the time when the work was begun, we were ready for our flight. So secretly had our two friends worked that no one in the camp guessed what they were doing. While Pitamakan and I sewed the skin inside the lodge, Raven had sat outside by the doorway, and in the sign-language told all inquirers that our hosts were away.

At dusk on a warm, still day, Young Otter came wading and towing the boat along the shore. His mother meanwhile had told his friends of what was to take place, and asked them to help us get away. When we came out of the lodge, there were more than a hundred young men and warriors waiting to escort us to the shore. No Kootenais were in sight, but before we arrived at the bank, they came hurrying from all directions, weapons in hand, and began arguing with the old Flathead chief.

"Come on! Come, quick!" Young Otter called from where he stood in shallow water, holding the boat. "They say that they have the right to shoot at you now."

Pitamakan and I ran forward, splashing up showers of water, but Raven was too dignified to hurry.

"Get in! Get in at that end!" Young Otter commanded. "I will take this end of the boat and protect you. They will not dare shoot for fear of hitting me."

We got in, and I realized that the boat was cranky. It was much too narrow for its length. Then came Raven.

He lifted a foot over the gunwale, placed it on the bottom, and with one hand grasping the rail, tried to use it as a lever to hoist himself over, just as one would do to vault a low fence. The result was disastrous; over went the boat, and all three of us floundered out into the shallow water, holding our guns high to keep them from the wet.

A loud shout of laughter went up from the crowd, but it was too anxious a time for any of us to laugh. Young Otter and I righted the boat, and held it while Raven got in; and I cautioned him to sit down and keep his hands off the sides. Then the rest of us took our places. Pitamakan and I dipped our paddles, and we were off. The Flatheads cheered, the Kootenais threatened us, and one of them fired a shot. The bullet spatted through the blade of Pitamakan's paddle.

At that the cheering turned to roars of anger. Glancing back, I saw the man struggling with several of our friends; then I paddled harder than ever. Out we went on the still water, and were soon beyond range of the enemies' guns. It was now getting dark, and I purposely changed our course several points toward the eastern shore. A moment or two later Young Otter exclaimed:—

"The Kootenais are leaving camp! I can see them hurrying along the shore. We had better keep out more in the lake until it is quite dark."

"I am purposely starting them in the wrong direction," I said. "We will land somewhere on the west shore of the lake."

"But that is not necessary," Young Otter objected. "You can land anywhere along here as soon as it is dark, and by morning you can be a long way on your homeward trail."

# THE QUEST OF THE FISH-DOG SKIN

Up to this time we had said nothing about the purpose of our journey, but now Raven told in a few words what we had set out to do. Young Otter listened intently, and uttered many exclamations of surprise and doubt.

"I can only wish you well, if you must go on," he said, "but I hope you will take my advice and go back straight to your own country. Think of the known enemies you have to the west—Snakes, Spokanes, and Nez Percés! Beyond them are many unknown tribes living along the Big River, some of whom eat the flesh of the people they capture. My friends, if you go down into that far country, you go to your death. Take my word, turn homeward now, this very night."

"I may not turn back unless I am warned to do so by my medicine," said Raven. "I have had no such warning; my dreams have all been favorable; we must go on."

"Yes, we must go on!" Pitamakan exclaimed.

"I will argue with you no longer," Young Otter said. "You insist upon going to your death. Well, I will help you to find it quickly. The trail to the west follows the outlet of this lake. I will direct you to it as soon as it is safe for us to change our course."

We paddled on in silence for some time. The night grew darker, and finally the glow in the western sky faded out, and all was black round us except the spot where the lodges of the camp glowed dimly with the pale yellow firelight that diffused itself through the leather skins.

Finally Young Otter gave the word, and I brought the boat round until its nose pointed to the southwest. After paddling for fully an hour in that direction, with a bright star for our guide, we came to the outlet, and landed on the south shore. In order to conceal the place of our landing, we weighted the boat with stones and sank it in five or six feet of water. Then Young Otter gave us instructions for following the trail to the lake of the Pend d'Oreilles, and the time for parting came. We tried to tell him how much we appreciated all that he and his mother had done for us, but somehow words failed. I had to turn away with a strange lump in my throat.

"Well, take courage! Take full courage!" he called after us.

"Ai! Ai! We do take courage," was our answer.

For several hundred yards the path was through a low growth of bushes, and Raven, leading, managed to keep on it. Then it entered the heavy forest, where the dim starlight did not penetrate, and within the length of a bowshot we were tumbling and floundering over logs and through the brush. We were not really lost, for the sullenly roaring river on our right was a sufficient guide. Nevertheless, we sat down and waited for the moon to rise; then, finding the trail, we went on and on, all through the night, and until late the next morning. The trail was always the same, through a forest of immense pines and heavy undergrowth, and was gloomy indeed to us of the open, sunlit plains.

Only one thing worried us: the possibility that the Kootenais might find our tracks in the sand where we had landed, and following, surprise us. The more we thought about this, the more we became convinced that the enemy were right then on our trail, and at last Raven, who had as usual done the least talking, stopped short, and said, "I have a feeling, a warning of coming danger. Follow me away from the trail."

# THE QUEST OF THE FISH-DOG SKIN

He had led us down to the river, and along in its shallows to a bare, rocky point, up which we climbed. When we came again to the trail, we jumped across it, and made our way up among the rocks for thirty or forty yards. There we hid behind a growth of brush, through which we could see any one who passed on the trail. We removed our packs, and opening them, made a hearty meal of dried meat and camass root that Young Otter's mother had provided for us.

We were very tired and sleepy. Raven ordered Pitamakan and me to lie down while he stood watch, and we had just stretched out for a comfortable rest, when from down the valley there came to us above the roar of the river the unmistakable sounds of approaching people—occasional shouts, barking of dogs and shrill neighing of horses. At that we re-primed our guns, and crouching down behind the brush, watched eagerly for the cause of the commotion.

We had not long to wait. There came into view down the trail a big, handsome, proud-looking Indian, dressed in clean buckskin, and riding a powerfully built pinto. A gun was laid across his saddle-bow, a beautiful otterskin bow-case and quiver was slung on his back, and a large shield hung suspended from his left arm. I felt at once that here was a chief, a man of mental as well as physical power, one who was accustomed to lead, and to be obeyed.

He was at the head of a long procession of riders, who came into view one by one and passed across the ridge into the timber again. Several hundred of them passed, all well-mounted and well-armed.

Then appeared the women and children and the aged, driving strings of pack-animals, and almost as well mounted as the warriors in the lead. Following them was band after band of loose stock, herded along by young men and boys, and behind came several hundred more fighting men, the rear guard of the long procession. They, too, passed on without a stop, and the sound of their voices and of the tramping of the horses was lost in the distance.

Drawing a long breath of relief, I turned to my companions. Raven's lips were moving, and I knew that he was praying. Presently he turned to us and said:—

"Always, always she is with me. This time I did not quite understand her, and thought she meant that the enemy were approaching us from behind. All is now well with us; the multitude have passed on, and the feet of many hundred horses have stamped out our footprints in the trail. Let us all now lie down and sleep."

"Who were they?" I asked.

"Blue Earth people, our bitter enemies," he replied. "They go, no doubt, to hunt on our plains and kill our buffalo."

Pitamakan laughed. "No doubt they do, but our people will find them. Many of those who passed us just now will never ride this trail again," he said.

So it was that I first saw the Kó-mo-ne-tup-pi, the Blue Earth people, or, as the Blackfeet name them, the Nez Percés: Noses Pierced.

We slept soundly there among the rocks and brush until night, then went down to the river and bathed, and ate another portion of our dried food. In mind I went over the incidents of the day again and again, always pausing to dwell on Raven's belief in the ever-guiding spirit of his dead wife. And I think that there was some excuse for me, a boy whose only associates were red people, if I began to have some faith in their superstitions.

When the moon was well up, we lifted our packs, climbed the ridge to the trail, and traveled on as fast as we could in the dim light of the forest. Occasionally we got a glimpse of the "Big Dipper," and so kept track of the passing of the night. Toward morning we entered a part of the forest where the trees grew more thickly than usual, and where the darkness was so intense that Raven, who was in the lead, had to feel out the trail step by step. The mixture of soft, loose earth and dead pine-needles completely muffled the tread of our moccasined feet. Suddenly, close ahead, a stick broke with a loud snap, and Raven stopped and almost instantly fired. The flash of the powder revealed some men on foot less than ten paces in front of us, and by the lariats and medicine-bags they carried, it was plain that we had run into a war party.

"Fall down beside me!" Raven commanded. We had no sooner done so than bow-cords twanged and arrows hissed above us.

# CHAPTER V

The flash of the gun blinded us for a moment. When we recovered from it, we tried to see our enemies, but the intense darkness hid even the faintest shadowy outline of them; overhead and all round, the branches of the firs were so thickly interlaced that not a ray of moonlight fell upon the forest floor. Moreover, after the flight of the arrow, there was not the least sound by which they could be traced; there was something uncanny about the stillness.

I lay close beside Raven on his right; Pitamakan was on his left. Presently I felt Raven rise on his hands and knees. Then he caught hold of my sleeve and jerked it, as he silently crept backward a few inches at a time. I understood what he meant, and keeping close to him, took good care not to place my knees or hands on any stick that would snap and betray our movements. We must have been a full half-hour creeping backward a distance of about a hundred yards.

At last, after a long stop, Raven rose to his feet, pulled us up, and getting hold of my hand, closed it on a fold of his robe, and held it there for a moment, as a sign that I was to retain the grasp. Then, making Pitamakan take hold of my capote in the same manner, he started away from the trail toward the river.

Our progress down the hill was as slow and as silent as the spreading of water on parched land. Fear went with us. At any moment we might collide with the enemy. There were many of them and only three of us, and undoubtedly they were intent on some plan to destroy us.

About two hundred yards below the trail we came to the edge of the heavy timber, and looked out not only on moonlight, but also on the first pale whiteness of dawn. Directly in front of us the ground, covered with tall grass, sloped down to the stream; a dense fog hid the banks and the surface of the river. We could see one another now. Raven loosened my hand from his robe, and motioned Pitamakan to let go of me. Then he went on with long, quick, and noiseless strides, and, leaving a plain, fresh trail in the dewy grass, we followed closely. When we were hidden by the fog, we stopped and listened intently for several minutes, but heard no suspicious sound.

Luckily, the river was shallow there, and taking care not to splash, we stepped into it and started downstream. After going some distance in this manner, we found that the water was getting deeper, and soon a brief lifting of the fog disclosed a cut rock wall ahead; under it the stream ran dark and swift. There we could not pass.

I supposed that Raven would lead us to the shore and down past the rocky point, but to my surprise he turned straight back upstream, and halted beside a huge pile of driftwood on a bar. At the outer end of it a large dead pine swung in the current, held to the pile only by two curved roots that were buried in it; at the other end several heavy splintered branches stuck four or five feet up into the air.

Raven motioned to us to stand where we were; he walked out on the trunk, and fastened his pack, weapons, and clothing to one of the branches. Then he came back, took our belongings, and fastened them to other branches. Although he had told us nothing of his plans, his intention was plain enough. While he was arranging our packs, we were noiselessly prying, lifting, and removing the brush that covered the roots of the tree. When we had cleared it away, we found that one of the roots was buried in the sand.

By pulling at it together, we soon freed it, and then, hanging to the tree and doing everything in our power to keep it from turning and burying our precious outfit in the water, off we went into the swift current.

Down past the rock wall we swept at a speed that bade fair quickly to carry us from that vicinity and to leave the enemy miles behind. But from the end of the point the current shot off toward the farther side of the river, and soon our craft ran into shallow water, scraped along the bottom, and stopped.

The fog was beginning to lift. Close ahead a brush-covered island loomed up; there was not a moment to waste. Snatching our things from the limbs, we hurried ashore, and crouching in the thickest part of the brush, shivering with cold, we put on our clothes, untied the packs with trembling fingers, and hungrily attacked the dried meat and roots.

By the time we had finished eating, the sun had come up and the fog had vanished. As the brush on the island was only waist-high, we crawled to the outer line of it, and lay watching the south shore of the river.

Until then we had been too anxious and miserable to talk. I now asked Raven how he had happened to discover the enemy in the dark. He seemed surprised at the question.

"Why, didn't you hear them? One of them said, 'Kaik, pisish,' plainly."

"Kaik, pisish! Kaik, pisish!" I repeated, and never forgot the words.

"Ai! Just that," he said absently. " 'Kaik, pisish' is Snake talk, and means, 'Yes, buffalo.' My father captured a Snake boy long ago, and I learned from him something of his language."

Another thought came to me. "Raven," I asked, "how about her? She did not warn you of the danger we were walking right into there in the dark!"

Pitamakan gave me a warning glance. I wished that I had not asked the question; but Raven was not offended, and answered, "Why, she was there in time. Neither of you heard the Snake's two words, but she caused me to hear them; and here we are, safe on this island."

At that moment a man appeared on the shore where we had entered the river an hour or two before. Then came another and another, until we had counted fourteen of them. They looked upstream and down; they waded out and examined the bottom of the shallow water; evidently they found places here and there where our feet had rubbed the slimy coating from the few stones that lay scattered on the sand. I remembered having stepped upon several.

Two of the enemy walked into the water; the rest followed on shore, looking carefully for any signs of our having returned to land. At last they neared the drift-pile on the bar.

"What we did there will not escape their eyes!" said Pitamakan.

He was right. In a moment or two those in the water called to the others, and they all gathered round the place and examined the end of the pile; then they started down the shore, hurried along the rock wall, and apparently without so much as a glance in our direction, kept on past us.

Usually, when a party takes to the water in hurried flight, each one grasps for himself the first piece of wood he can find that will enable him to float or swim alongside it and keep his weapons dry. No doubt that is what they thought we had done.

As they passed, not a hundred yards from our hiding-place, we had a good look at them, and because I was accustomed to the tall and well-dressed Indians of the plains, the appearance of these surprised me. Almost without exception they were short and heavy-set. They wore shabby, dingy buckskin leggings, tattered and worn buffalo-robes, and wolf-head skins for caps; and their uncombed and tangled hair fell loosely round their shoulders and partly concealed their faces. Not one of them had a gun; some had no shield, but all carried a bow and quiver of arrows.

The party kept on down the shore, and soon disappeared round a bend of the river. Raven thought that, as they were probably bound for the plains on a horse-stealing raid, they would not go very far in search of us. We decided to remain where we were until night, and then, by pushing the pine tree out into deep water and drifting with it, to try to get back to the south shore.

Pitamakan and I talked about the wretched appearance of the Snakes, and Raven informed us that all were not like those who had just passed. There were three tribes, or bands, of the nation, he said, Shin-i-dai-kas, as they called themselves, meaning Dog-Eaters; Wah-an-i-kas, or Fish-Eaters; and the Pan-ah-tis, or Thieves. The Dog-Eaters, he said, were the largest of the three tribes. They were tall, cleanly people, well-dressed, and owners of immense bands of horses. They lived on the great plains of the Snake and Salmon rivers, where there were many buffalo. The Fish-Eaters were also a large tribe, but fat, dirty, and poor; they spent all their time on the rivers, catching and eating fish. The worst tribe was that of the Thieves. They wandered in small bands, and stole from every one, even other tribes of their own nation. Although they were very poor and unclean, they were the best hunters of all, for they were able to crawl almost anywhere without being seen, and so closely to imitate the calls of animals and birds that they would come to them. There was no doubt that those we had seen were members of the Thief tribe.

We slept by turns during the day. As soon as it was dusk we got ready to leave the island. We found that a shallow bar extended from the upper end to the north shore of the river; so we abandoned the pine tree, and wading across, continued our journey on that side. It was hard, slow work, stumbling through the forest and along the shore in the dark, and during the night we could not have traveled more than eight or ten miles. When day began to break we made a raft of driftwood and birch withes, crossed to the south side of the river, and returned to the trail. The dust in it showed the marks of barefooted men traveling east; evidently the Thieves were too poor to afford moccasins, or their women were too lazy to make them.

Instead of waiting until dusk, we resumed our journey at noon that day, and began hunting as we went along, for we had eaten the last of the dried food. We shot with bow and arrow at several deer, but missed them. Late in the afternoon, Pitamakan killed a young doe that crossed the trail close ahead of us.

We were very hungry. Dragging the animal down to the river, we soon had some fat meat broiling over a fire of driftwood. Raven stood guard on the trail until the meal was cooked, whereupon we put out the fire and went far back into the thick timber above the trail to feast.

After eating rib after rib of the well-browned and tender meat, we had no zest for the trail through the dark and endless forest, and soon we rolled into our blankets, and slept soundly all night long.

From that point on we traveled only by day. The trail ran straight down the valley, cutting across the bends of the swift, green river, and day after day there was the same monotonous vista of dark and silent woodland broken by stretches of the hurrying stream.

Once we paused to look at a cataract, which I think must be the one now known as Thompson's Falls. Later we skirted the base of a high range of mountains, the Coeur d'Alenes, that long years afterward became famous for their mines.

It was on the tenth morning after leaving Flathead Lake that we came out of the forest into some grassy parks, where the wind blew strong from the west. After we had crossed these and had passed through a fringe of cotton-woods, the great lake of the Pend d'Oreilles lay before us. The green waves broke angrily on a granite-strewn shore; wooded islands dotted the water here and there, and in places wooded hills rose one after another from the shore to the precipitous slopes of high mountain ranges. We had completed the second great division of our journey.

From what we could see of the shore of the lake, the river came in at about the centre of the eastern side, and went out at the south-western end. We knew that the outlet ran into the big river we sought; so we turned southward, and passed through meadow after meadow that skirted the shore.

Many water-birds kept continually flying over our heads—ducks, gulls, and pelicans. Raven declared that the pelicans were of bad omen, since they were descendants of the monstrous dagger-billed birds that had killed all the children of the Sun and Moon except one, Morning Star.

After telling us that, he muttered to himself for some time, and at last said that we had better stop and make a sacrifice to the people and creatures of the deep lake waters. Untying his pack, he took from it a small buckskin medicine, or sacred pouch, and from that a smaller one that was ornamented with a narrow band of red porcupine-quill embroidery. Into this he put a wisp of dried sweet-grass, a strip of otterskin, a package of vermilion, and a sacred stone called "i-nis'kim" (buffalo stone). Then, tying the neck of the pouch securely, he threw it out into the breakers, and prayed:—

"Listen, O you Above People! Listen, you people and strange creatures of the deep, dark waters! And you, sacred

70

ones of the land and the air, listen! Have pity on us, all of you! Help us; give us of your power, that we may go safe through this land of many enemies, and, finding that which we seek, return in safety to the lodges of our kinsmen. We are poor, but we sacrifice to you the most sacred things we have. Look with favor on our gift and preserve us from the dangers that are on every hand."

"Ai! Have pity on us!" Pitamakan echoed, fervently. There were tears in his eyes, and my own were misty; the grace and impressiveness, the sincerity and faith with which Raven had made the prayer would have moved a much sterner heart than mine.

"She told me to do it," he informed us as he led on; and there was renewed energy in his steps, and on his face was an expression of perfect satisfaction that we in a measure shared.

At midday we came to a deep bay, and at the foot of it saw the tops of some lodges sticking above the fringe of willows near the shore. Some children were playing on the sandy beach, and a woman passed near them, carrying a bundle of sticks on her back. We drew back into the brush instantly, in the fear that some of them might have discovered us; but evidently we had not been seen.

"I think that they are Pend d'Oreilles, a few lodges of the tribe that chose to remain here instead of going out on the plains," said Raven.

"Ai! That may well be," Pitamakan agreed. "I wish now that we had talked with the old chief of the tribe before starting on this quest; he might have told us many helpful things."

That had been my thought more than once since crossing the backbone. We had been too greedy for the reward for the medicine-skin, too anxious to start before any one else should start.

"Well, we will just lie here until dark, and then see who these people are," Raven declared. "If they prove to be River People, we will camp with them for a night or two."

We remained where we were for the rest of the day, and saw people coming and going on the beach. When it was quite dark we moved cautiously toward the lodges, which were all illuminated by the cheerful little fires within. As we listened to the talk and laughter of the people, we hoped that they would prove to be friends; Pitamakan and I were starving for good cheer and the company of our kind. As for Raven, I doubt if he gave a thought to anything except his ghostly communings with the shadow of his lost wife.

As there were many dogs round the lodges, we halted at a safe distance from them, and listened intently to hear the language that the people used. None of us understood Pend d'Oreille, but Raven had heard it enough to know when it was being spoken.

"They are the River People," he said, after a moment, and then shouted in Blackfoot:—

"River People! Arrived here are Blackfeet friends!"

As soon as he began to shout, the dogs made a rush toward us and drowned his words with their fierce barking; women screamed and children squalled; men shouted to one another as, with weapons in hand, they rushed outside. After Raven had repeated his words several times, some one at last understood him, and answered:—

"Ai! Ai! Ki-ka! Ki-ka!" (Yes! Yes! Wait! Wait!)

The men quieted the dogs and came toward us, and we

advanced to meet them. All the time Raven was proudly proclaiming that we were Blackfeet friends. We met in the darkness, and a quavering voice that indicated old age greeted us in Blackfoot, but brokenly, as was natural.

"We River People glad," this old man said. "Come, Blackfeet, our lodges enter."

They escorted us to the largest of the thirty lodges in the camp. This was the home of the old man who spoke Blackfoot, and he gave us seats of honor on each side of him. Several leaders of the camp also came in and sat down, eager to hear our news. Not a woman or child was in sight; they had all taken to the bush as soon as the dogs gave the alarm. But the women who belonged in this lodge soon returned, and at a word from the old man, began to prepare a meal for us.

Two of them were very old; the other, who was not more than twenty years of age, was decidedly handsome. She wore a tight-fitting skull-cap made like a basket of finely woven grass, striped blue and red. I had never seen one before; but later I found that these people made beautiful baskets, pouches, bags, and panniers of grass, some of which were so closely woven that they would hold water for a long time.

We were no sooner seated than our host filled and lighted his pipe for a peace-smoke with us. The manner in which he passed it to Raven was so strange and tantalizing that it was all I could do to keep from laughing outright. He presented the pipestem first to him, but as Raven grasped it and put it to his lips, forbade him to draw a whiff, and after a moment took the pipe back. This he did three times, and then handing it to him a fourth time, said:—

"Now, smoke. You are a man, because you can resist taking that which you crave, even when it is in your mouth."

Raven took a few whiffs, passed the pipe on, and related all the news we had. When he told of the River People's coming to us on the plains, with their horses heavily loaded with buffalo meat and hides, his listeners were so pleased that several of them hurried out to carry the good tidings to the other lodges.

Our meal was now set before us: large pieces of broiled fish, some camass, and bitterroot, boiled, and a quantity of fresh huckleberries. The fish was the most delicious I had ever tasted. Raven called it the big spotted fish of the other side. Long afterward I learned that the right name for it was salmon.

The old man asked what our mission on the west side was, and looked very solemn when Raven told him. When he translated the answer to the others, they also looked gravely and doubtfully at one another, and said a few words that we could not understand. But the expression of their faces made us uneasy; and Pitamakan asked the old man what our chance was of getting the medicine-skin.

"We will talk about that to-morrow," he replied. "To-night we make you welcome among us; we will have a dance."

He sent a woman to invite certain persons, and soon they came trooping in, young men and women, and a few old men, who brought drums. The dance was much like the woman's dance of the Blackfeet; the men and women were on opposite sides of the lodge. In time to the singing and drumming of the old people, the dancers rose and danced in two lines, advancing and retreating repeatedly for a few minutes; then they all sat down and rested for a time after which the performance was repeated. I thought it monotonous, but Pitamakan enjoyed it. As usual, Raven sat quietly, with the old far-away look in his eyes.

I was glad when the dancers were at last dismissed and we were permitted to make our beds. As we stretched out for the night, Pitamakan asked the old man why these lodges of the tribe had not gone out to the plains with the main body. He replied that a part of the people had been too old to travel, and that the others, their sons and daughters, had stayed to take care of them.

Soon all was quiet in the lodge and in the camp. I lay on the inside of the couch of deer and elk skins, covered myself with my blanket, and enjoyed the comfort. Although very tired, I was strangely wide awake, and watched the dying fire for a long time after all the others were fast asleep.

As the last of the cottonwood coals began to dim and to turn to white ash, a dog close outside gave a low, whimpering, questioning growl, but I could hear nothing that might have aroused his suspicions. He growled again, more assertively; others joined in the same low key, and in a moment every dog in camp began barking furiously, and in a way that expressed great fear.

"Wake up!" I cried, nudging Pitamakan in the side, "Raven! And you, River People, wake up!"

I did not need to call again; on all sides of the camp rose shrill yells. Within the lodges women and children screamed and cried, and men shouted to one another. Several shots were fired; I heard three arrows rip into our lodge one after another, and felt the prick of one in my left shoulder.

"Lie down flat!" Raven called, in a sharp voice, to Pitamakan and me. We dropped, and fairly hugged the ground.

75

## CHAPTER VI

The old man shouted to his women, as I learned later, to lie close to the ground and keep still. The men in the other lodges gave the same orders; and after a moment not a sound was to be heard from the River People. But the enemy about us continued to yell, discharge their arrows, and fire an occasional shot into the lodges. Two dogs that had been shot yelped with pain, and all the rest kept up a furious barking.

"Come! We must do something," Raven said. "Crawl as close to the ground as you can, and follow me."

Dragging our guns, Pitamakan and I felt our way to him. He led us to the back of the lodge, and by pulling a couple of pins, raised the lodge skin and let us pass under it.

"Now, watch, and when you see the flash of a gun, shoot at it!" he ordered, when he had joined us outside. "Then crawl away as fast as you can round to the other side of the lodge, and be ready to shoot again."

We had not long to wait for a shot. Right in front of us, less than thirty yards away, an old *fuke* belched a stream of fire, and almost at the same instant the reports of our three guns sounded. A piercing scream out in the brush told us that one of our bullets had found its mark. It was too much for Pitamakan's excitable nature; he yelled the Blackfoot war cry:—

"Wo-ke-hai! Wo-ke-hai! I-ka-ki-mat Siks-uh-kah!" (Now, then! Now, then! Take courage, Blackfeet!)

For the life of me, I could not help shouting, too, and Raven joined in with thundering voice. A flight of arrows came hurtling toward us, but we were already moving round to the other side of the lodge, and we escaped them. When we passed close to the rear of it, the old man was crawling out under the lodge skin.

"I have no weapon but my knife, and I am very weak," he said, "but I am going to be as brave as you Blackfeet, and try to encourage my people."

"You talk right," Raven replied. "When we shoot and yell again, call your people. Urge them to come out and shoot and yell."

At that moment there rose a fearful cry of pain, evidently from the very centre of the camp; then the enemy on all sides shouted louder than ever, let fly more arrows, and fired several shots from their guns. We shot at the blaze of the one nearest us, and again gave the Blackfoot cry.

The old man also shouted, and at the same time harangued his people. The effect was at once apparent: answering shouts came from all parts of the camp; bow-strings twanged and guns spit fire among the lodges.

Meanwhile, we three were reloading our weapons as fast as we could. Before we had them ready, however, the enemy ceased yelling; then the River People gradually

77

became quiet, and soon not a sound was to be heard except the moaning whimper of one of the wounded dogs.

We listened, trying in vain to discover some movement of the enemy; at last Raven said that they must have gone. The old man agreed with him, and asked him what he thought we ought to do.

"We can do nothing except lie here ready for them, and wait for the morning light," said Raven. "Tell your men to do that."

"It shall be as you Blackfeet say," the old man replied. "You are the true war people. What should we have done to-night without you? It must be that the Great Coyote sent you to us."

He shouted the orders, and from all parts of the camp came the answer: "Ah-ah! Ah-ah! E-hest! E-hest!" (Yes! Yes! Good! Good!)

Except for the sound of owls calling—too often to be natural—we heard no disturbing noises during the rest of the night. The old man remarked that those who did the hooting were birds without feathers. But the sounds did not last long, and gradually died out in the distance.

With the first light of the morning, we looked gradually before us. Little by little the reddening sky dissolved the shadows and lighted our surroundings; fortunately, there was no underbrush, and no place near in which the enemy might lie hidden.

"They have gone away," Raven said to the old man, "but of course they have taken all your horses."

The chief laughed. "They got none of our horses," he replied. "We sent them with our people to the plains, to be loaded with buffalo hides and dry meat for our winter comfort."

Just then a commotion arose in the centre of the camp. "They say that an enemy is dead there," the old man announced.

We ran to where the crowd had collected. There, flat on his back, lay a heavy-set man, with coarse features and matted hair. He was clad only in worn leather leggings and breechclout. In his breast was a wide, blood-stained slit where he had been knifed. On one side lay a worn and tattered elkskin robe; his left hand still clutched a bow. He was a Snake—apparently one of the Thief tribe.

"Who killed him?" Raven asked; the old chief repeated the question in his own language. No one answered. He repeated the question in a louder voice; still there was no answer. Although every man of the camp was present by that time, not one of them claimed the honor. All at once Pitamakan laughed as if he had heard a joke.

"What is the matter with you?" Raven asked, looking at him sternly. "Are you going crazy?"

"No, no!" he replied, as soon as he could control himself. "Can't you see how it was? Two of them sneaked into the camp, and each mistook the other for an enemy. Yes, that is the way it happened; this man was killed by his brother."

Pitamakan and I then made a bee-line to the timber where the scream had followed our first shots; we found much blood spattered on the ground, but that was all. The wounded man had managed to get away, or had been helped to escape by his companions.

Several of the young men left at once, to find out what had become of the enemy; about noon they reported that the Thieves had gone straight east on the river trail. There seemed to be no end to the war parties that were heading for the Blackfoot Country.

The River People had shown us marked kindness upon our arrival in their camp; the events of the night had increased their respect for us. We could easily see this in their attitude toward Raven; they told him that if it had not been for his brave stand, the enemy would have come in among the lodges, and no doubt would have made a big killing. Anything they had, the old chief told him—furs, weapons, sacred medicines—was his for the asking.

Raven replied that he had done nothing worth talking about, and wanted nothing. But the women did not take him at his word; in the course of the morning they brought us some finely tanned elkskins for new leggings, and several pairs of moccasins.

All this time we recalled how strangely these people had acted when they learned that we were bound for the mouth of the Big River, and we waited anxiously for the council that the night before they had promised to hold. Our host, however, spent most of the day going from one lodge to another, and it was not until after dark that the talk took place. They told us then that to go on was surely to go to our death; they said that along the Big River lived many white men, who carried on a terrible war against the tribes of Indians in that region, and that it would be impossible for us to escape both sides.

"But I am white; the white men would not harm me," I said.

The old chief looked at me pityingly, as one looks at a little child, and replied, "They would kill you even more quickly than they would kill an Indian. Nothing you could say would make them believe that you were not allied with the tribes against them."

"But we are of the Blackfeet," I argued. "The whites would have to admit that we who are Indians of the plains have nothing whatever to do with their wars."

"You are wrong!" he exclaimed. "To them all Indians are merely marks for their bullets. Why, they would not even give you a chance to explain! You and your two friends would be shot at sight."

"Yes," said Raven. "We could expect nothing except bullets from the whiteskins."

"You all talk foolishly," Pitamakan declared. "The white soldiers are nothing; they have ears that don't hear and eyes that don't see. It is easy enough to avoid them; and as for the tribes of that country, well, they can be no worse than our enemies elsewhere—"

The old chief interrupted him. "Some of the people along that river make captives of their enemies. They fatten them with plenty of food, and then kill and eat them," he said.

There was much more talk, and in the course of it, one after another of the old men advised us to turn back; the old chief interpreted to us what they said. Pitamakan and I did most of the arguing in favor of our going on. Raven, however, ended the council. "There is truth in what all of you say," he declared, "but this is not a matter to be decided right now, here before the fire. I must dream about it, and consult my medicine. By morning I shall know what is best to do."

The council broke up then, and because it was feared that their enemy might return and make another attack, Pitamakan and I, leaving Raven to his dreams, went out with a number of young men to guard the camp. The night passed quietly, however, and soon after daybreak we returned to the lodge. The women were preparing something to eat; the old chief was having an early smoke, and Raven was making up his pack.

When we took our seats, he said, "We will go on. Our shadows were together last night; she pointed to the west, and these were her words: 'If you keep on going, down on the far water you will find—' "

He was silent for a moment, and then continued, "Now that is all I heard. I awoke; it was daylight, and the women here were starting the fire. But it is plain what she would have said—"

"Yes, yes!" Pitamakan eagerly broke in. " 'You shall find—' Find what? Why, the fish-dog skin, of course."

"Ai, just that," Raven agreed. Turning to the old man, who had been attentively listening, he added, "You will tell us just what way to go from here?"

"You shall know all that we know about it," he replied. "But that is little. None of the River People have ever been farther than the falls where the People of the Falls* catch fish. It was from one of them that the medicine-man got the sacred skin that you saw."

The kind old man plainly showed his concern over our decision to continue the quest. After the morning meal, he insisted that we should take a medicine-sweat with him, and when the hot rocks in the low, dark sweat-lodge were sprinkled and the steam rose from them, he earnestly prayed to the Big Coyote and other gods of the River People to have pity on us, and to preserve us from all enemies.

*People of the Falls—the Spokanes.

82

# THE QUEST OF THE FISH-DOG SKIN

When the ceremony was finished and we were back in the home lodge, he gave each of us a bit of sacred medicine securely tied in a piece of buckskin. He said that if we did not open the packets, or do anything else to anger the spirit of the medicine, we should have good luck as long as we carried them.

The people now came crowding in from all parts of the camp with offerings of food, dry meat and roots, enough to have loaded several packhorses. Women of the lodge had already filled our packs with all we could carry, and the others were plainly disappointed that we could not use their gifts.

We had thought that the westward trail from this point would be beside the river that ran out of the lake; but the old chief told us that this outlet ran due north from the lake for many days' travel, and then turned to the west and southwest. On a bare spot of ground he drew a rude map that showed the country as far as he knew it.

Our course, he pointed out, was to follow an old trail running west of south to the falls of the People of the Falls. From there we were to keep on for several days in the same general direction, until we reached the River of the Snakes; by following that, we should come at last to the Big River. Beyond that point none of them had ever been; they believed, however, that the Big Salt Lake was not many days' travel farther west.

The old chief's parting advice was to save our dry food for a time of want, and to avoid the People of Pointed Hearts,* who lived on another large lake and on a river not far to the south. Then we put on our packs, and started

* The Coeur d'Alene Indians.

83

again on the long trail. As was the Indian custom, all the people of the camp silently watched us go.

The trail ran close to the shore of our lake as far as the southern end of it; thence it turned due south along a small stream that came from the low mountains. On top of the divide the trail, which at no time was plain, ceased entirely. But that did not worry us; the timber was open and the traveling good. Somewhere ahead ran the Pointed Heart River; by following that we would come to the falls. There was not much big game on this divide, but grouse were plentiful, and during the day Pitamakan killed enough of them for our evening and morning meals.

About three o'clock the next afternoon we descended into a broad valley, and as we had found no water since early morning, and were therefore very thirsty, we hurried across it toward the stream that we knew must be at the other side. As usual, Raven was leading. All at once he stopped so suddenly that I almost stumbled over him. Right in front of us was a broad, much-used trail; fresh tracks of people and horses traveling both ways showed that we were not far from a large camp.

"We must hide ourselves at once!" Raven exclaimed.

"Well, make for the river," said Pitamakan. "My throat is fire."

One after another we jumped the trail, in order that our parflèche-soled moccasins would leave no telltale prints in the dust. Faster and faster Raven led us, until at last he broke into a stealthy run. In a few minutes we came to the edge of a long, narrow, grassy park, and saw on the far side of it a number of lodges. People were walking about among them, and several hundred horses that had evidently been driven to water were straggling back to grass.

One glance at the scene was enough for us. We turned back to recross the trail, but stopped short when we heard singing in that direction. Near us was a thicket of rose-brush, and regardless of thorns, we scrambled into it and lay down. A moment later four horsemen, one of whom had a large beaver tied to his saddle, rode by on their way to the camp. They were heavy-set, broad-faced men, careless of their hair, and poorly dressed in buckskins and worn old blankets. Two carried guns; the others bow and arrows.

As soon as they had gone, we settled ourselves more comfortably in the brush, prepared to remain there until dark. In a short time a man and three women came from the park into the timber in front of us, and collecting a few dry sticks, laid them for a fire not fifty yards from where we lay. Instead of using a steel and a flint-pouch that dangled from the belt of one of the women, the man lighted the fire by means of a bow fire-drill; that, and the fact that none of them carried food, showed that some kind of a medicine performance was about to take place.

As soon as the fire was burning well, the women seated themselves on one side of it; the man sat cross-legged on the other side, and laid a small, red-painted buckskin pouch in front of him. Judged by the standard of the proud and particular Blackfeet, all of them were ill-clothed and unkempt, and their short, heavy persons were not pleas-ing to us.

From the fire the man presently raked some coals; on these he sprinkled a few pinches of a substance that he took from the red pouch, and as the stuff burned, he held his hands in the smoke, and then rubbed them on his arms and chest. At the same time he began a low, weirdly plaintive song, in which the women joined.

This lasted for several minutes, and then the man suddenly changed the song to one that was shrill and jerky. While they sang, they held their arms bent close in front of their bodies, and moved their hands in a way to imitate the paws of squirrels. The motions seemed so ridiculous for grown people to make that I could not help smiling.

But Raven and Pitamakan could see no fun in the ceremony. To them the medicine practices even of an enemy were serious and sacred matters that were not to be derided. I noticed that their faces were very solemn, and that they watched the performance with intense interest.

The second song lasted fully five minutes, and ceased as abruptly as the first had done. The man drew fresh coals from the fire, sprinkled them with stuff from the red pouch, and, all the time praying fervently, again purified himself with smoke. Suddenly he dropped forward on all fours, and swiftly, in time with the shrill, jerky song that the women again started, crept directly toward us for four or five yards. Then the song came to one of its abrupt pauses; he put his face so close to the ground that his nose was buried in it, and at the same time the women gave a long-drawn-out cry, or rather squeak, "Tsik!"

The man stuck his face in the soft ground four times, and each time he raised it, his eyes seemed to shine brighter than before, until they looked like two greenish-black balls of fire. Immediately after the fourth time, both he and the women raised their hands to imitate a squirrel's paws, and squeaked "Tsik!" four times, sharply turning their heads and gazing in succession to the right, to the left, at the sky, and at the ground. To me this was all increasingly funny.

If you ever saw a squirrel or a chipmunk suddenly pause in its wanderings, smell of the ground, and then frantically paw the earth from round a crisp rootlet or a buried nut, you will know what the man did next. The women, raising again the jerky song, crept swiftly past the fire, and holding up their hands, squatted round him. Suddenly the man, with his perspiring face thickly coated with earth, straightened up; the women abruptly ceased singing, bent toward him, and together squeaked "Tsik!"

That was too much for me; I laughed aloud, and then shuddered with sudden fright at what I had done.

## CHAPTER VII

"You are crazy!" (Ki-tut´saps!") Raven hissed in my ear, as he cocked his gun.

Apparently all of the little group heard the laugh; they straightened up and looked round them and at one another as if they could hardly believe their ears. The man spoke, and some of the women shook their heads; then one of them pointed straight at the rose-brush thicket where we lay. At that he got up on his feet, and, talking angrily, came toward us. The women rose and followed him. He had evidently come out with his family to go through his medicine-squirrel ceremony in secret, and he now believed that some of his people were spying on him and making fun of it.

It needed only a glance to take in all this, and then I saw Raven raise his gun. There came over me a horror of seeing an unarmed man shot down, and as if by accident, I lurched against him and tilted the muzzle of the weapon down just as it was discharged. Pitamakan did not even raise his gun. He grabbed up his pack and dashed back in the direction we had come; and for once, regardless of his dignity, Raven came along with us as fast as he could run.

Through the smoke from his gun, I had seen the women fall back and tumble over one another; when, after getting hold of my pack, I next looked that way, they were all up and running toward the park. The man was well in the lead, and in his efforts to rouse the camp, was shouting loudest of all. I doubt whether any of them took time to get a good look at us, or to notice in which direction we ran.

Taking good care to jump the trail, we raced back up the slope of the valley, and did not stop until we had placed a couple of miles between us and the rose-brush patch. A thick growth of young balsams offered a good hiding-place; panting, and almost choking from want of water, we dived into it.

It was an anxious watch that we kept there until night. Every moment we expected to see the enemy come sneaking in a long line up the hill; but none came, nor did we even hear them. Probably they thought that we were the scouts of a big war party, and at once rounded up their horses and got ready to defend their camp.

As we lay in the balsams, the usually silent Raven spoke many times about the medicine ceremony that we had witnessed. It seemed to have made a deep and unpleasant impression upon him.

"There's no doubt it was powerful medicine he was making," he said, "and we interrupted it. That may prove unlucky for us; he may be able to make it do us great harm."

Pitamakan also took that view of it; and when, in the darkness, we started again, both of them were feeling low-spirited. My efforts to make light of the matter had failed.

# THE QUEST OF THE FISH-DOG SKIN

It was hard traveling in the dark woods; but when, striking the valley some distance below the camp, we came into more open country, we found park after park of fine grass where the starlight was bright enough to light our way. As soon as it was safe, we turned down to the river, and were surprised to find that it was of considerable size. The water was very cold, and we drank so much that it actually made us shiver. I proposed that we should open our packs and eat a meal of dry food, but Raven would not permit it; he said that we must keep what we had for a time when we were really starving.

During the night we traveled many miles down the valley; but though we often struck the big trail, we took care never to step in it. At daybreak we were beside an unusually quiet reach of the river, and we therefore made a raft of driftwood and crossed as quickly as we could to the south side. Not far back from the shore we found another trail. As there were no marks of travel on it, we decided that we could hunt and cook without being disturbed by the Pointed Hearts. Grouse were plentiful; out of three or four coveys, my companions soon killed enough for several meals.

We roasted them over smokeless coals of dry cottonwood bark, and after eating three apiece, moved on for about a mile, and lay down for the day in some willows that bordered the stream.

After our experience with the Pointed Hearts, we hid in the brush by the river during the day, and traveled at night. The meat of a young white-tail deer that Pitamakan shot with an arrow made us rich in food again.

Near daybreak, after the third night, the deep roaring warned us that the falls of the river were not far away. We hurried on through fine open timber, and soon after sunrise looked out on a prairie dotted with small, rocky hillocks and buttes covered with pines.

Close ahead the deep green river rushed through a channel of rough, dark rocks, and dropped over a high ledge. This was the fall (now known as Spokane Falls) to which the River People had directed us; we soon learned that it was the upper one of two falls.

As we saw no People of the Falls, or any lodges, or horses or dogs, or life of any kind, we could not resist the temptation to move on little by little, from tree to tree and from boulder to boulder, until we were directly opposite the big drop in the channel. From that point there was a good view of the country for miles round; there were no rising spirals of smoke from early lighted lodge-fires, or any signs of human life.

There were evidences, however, that this was a great camping-place; in all directions the ashes of hundreds of lodge-fires, together with broken lodge-poles, fallen fish-racks, old bones, discarded moccasins, and clothing littered the ground. We spent part of the morning in looking at the two falls, and in making a circle in search of the trail to the River of the Snakes. It proved to be a very faint one; evidently it had not been used for several seasons.

The following morning we began the next stage of our journey, from the falls to the River of the Snakes. All day we traveled through a high, broken country, with many lakes, in which wild fowl abounded. We killed and roasted enough geese to make a welcome change of fare for several days. On the fourth morning after leaving the falls we came to a small stream that flowed southward in a valley of rough, volcanic rock. Toward evening we reached the junction of this stream with a much larger one, and followed that until it entered a deep cañon, where we camped for the night. Except a few willows, there was no wood in this region, and it took us a long time to collect enough to roast some ducks that we had killed during the day.

The next morning, as we did not like the looks of the dark cañon, and had lost the old trail, we climbed out on the east side, and after traveling for several hours parallel with the gash, came suddenly to the edge of a hill overlooking a large river, which was without doubt the Snake. The River People had described it as a swift stream of whitish muddy water that flowed for most of the way deep down between walls of rock; and that is what we saw before us.

There was a trail here, and when we had made sure that there were no people in the narrow valley, we descended into it, and went down the bottom to the mouth of the cañon that we had been following.

From the long rows of racks for drying fish that we found on the shore, it was plain that here was a favorite camping-place for the Indians of the country; and evidently they had not long been gone, for the ashes in the fire-places were still light and fluffy. The well-worn horse trail that crossed the river showed that the camp had moved southward.

We went on, following the course of the river, and toward night found our way blocked by a high cliff. As it was too late to go back and look for a way out of the cañon, we prepared to camp where we were until morning. The spring rise had left driftwood lodged among the rocks, and we dragged some of it up on level ground and built a fire. In this deep, deserted bend of the river, where there were no trails or any signs of human beings, it seemed safe enough to do so.

We had not shot any game during the day, and for the first time since leaving the River People we made a meal of some of the dried meat and roots with which they had stuffed our packs. The night was cold. A north wind blew up the river; it whistled among the crags above and washed the swift water into a choppy sea that beat noisily against the rocky shore. A large boulder screened the little fire from the force of the blasts. Shielding our faces with our hands and enjoying the heat, we sat bowed over close before it. But we were far from being happy; although I would not have acknowledged it for anything, I was regretting that I had started on this far quest, and wishing that I was safe in Fort Benton with my Uncle Wesley and Tsistsaki.

Pitamakan gloomily remarked that above us among the crags ghosts were crying; that they often came with strong winds, and shrieked and whistled and wailed about the camp-fires of people, because they themselves were nothing but shadows, and could no longer feel the pleasant heat of fire.

"But let's take courage," he said. "Let's cheer up. Of course we are going to find the fish-dog skin and get safe home with it." And to help, he began to sing the song of the wolf.

He was about half through it when I thought that I heard a faint "tunk" of a rock being overturned, and looking over my shoulder, I saw a number of big, wide-faced, loose-haired Indians stealthily advancing toward us.

I yelled, and grasped the gun beside me, and at that instant I felt a blow on the shoulder that almost knocked me into the fire. I struggled to rise, but several men on my back held me down, and many hands seized my wrists.

For a moment there was great confusion. My companions were struggling with their captors; Pitamakan was yelling with rage and terror, Raven was calling frantically upon "her" for help, and the enemy were talking excitedly one to another. Some one took the knife from my belt, and then my captors freed me.

I sat up, and saw that my companions had done the same. There we sat, breathing hard as the result of our futile struggles. Our captors—there were more than thirty of them—stood round us and round our little fire. They looked down at us and talked and laughed, while their chief examined the contents of our packs. He divided the different articles in them, and kept my fine rifle and the largest share of the things for himself.

I had never thought I should see such a disgusting lot of Indians as those were. Their teeth were worn down and yellow; few wore any clothing except a shirt and a breech-clout, and a short deerskin or fur robe; and their big, wide, bare feet were fit supports for their broad, heavy bodies. Not more than half of them carried guns; the rest had short, heavy bows and full quivers of arrows.

But I was too much concerned about our terrible predicament to give them more than a passing glance. I turned to my companions, and saw that they were now looking as unconcerned as if this were an every-day occurrence.

"Whatever happens, be brave," Pitamakan said to me. "Show them that the Blackfeet can die without a cry of fear."

"You think, then, that these are eaters of people?" I asked.

"Of course they are," Raven said, "or they would have

shot us instead of capturing us. No doubt we shall be taken to their camp, and fattened for a tribal feast."

The chief ordered his men to freshen the fire, and then, after attracting Raven's attention, tried by using the sign-language, in which he was far from proficient, to learn something about us. But after one scowling glance, Raven deliberately turned and looked steadily into the fire, and Pitamakan and I at once followed his example.

At that the man said something to his companions that made them all laugh, and caused us to grow hot with resentment. I have learned that there are few things more trying than to be the object of talk and jokes in a language that you cannot understand.

The supply of driftwood did not last long; when the last sticks were laid on the fire, each of us was tied to one of our captors with the thongs of our packs, and the whole party lay down to rest. Since our captors had taken our extra blankets, we were soon shivering from cold; but the half-naked enemy, most of whom were only partly covered by their short robes, slept and snored all round us in apparent comfort. It was an anxious and miserable night.

At the first light of day the chief roused the party; in a few minutes our captors unfastened our thongs, and guarding us carefully, started away up the river. But we did not have far to go; less than two hundred yards above our camp we came to three long dugout canoes tied to the bank in a sheltered eddy of the stream.

We must have shown our surprise and chagrin at seeing them, for the whole crowd laughed and jeered as they hustled us into them, Pitamakan and I into the rear one, and Raven into the one in front of it. The third and smallest canoe, with only six men in it, was pushed off first, and went rapidly ahead of the others, no doubt to act as a scout.

"Last night we thought only of trails by land, and we were fools," Pitamakan declared. "We should have remembered what the River People told us—that the tribes here travel oftener by water than by land."

"Yes, and if only we had not built the fire, we should now be safe," I said.

The speed at which we went down the river amazed us. Every one of our captors used a paddle. Although the canoes were broad at the bow, they were thin, graceful craft, and they drew very little water. During the day we ran a number of rapids; several times it seemed impossible for the canoe to live among the rocks and the leaping, foaming water. But the paddlers showed not the slightest concern; by the stolid and placid expression of their faces, it was evident that they had made the passage more than once, and had no fear.

At the foot of one long stretch of rapids we passed five Indian huts that were shaped somewhat like an A tent, and built of thin split shakes about twelve feet long. The scout canoe had stopped there ahead of us, and now came alongside, bringing a woven grass pouch filled with dried salmon pounded fine. Each man was allowed to take a double handful of it, and although the stuff neither smelled nor tasted good, Pitamakan and I managed to eat our portions.

Late in the afternoon the men in the front canoe signaled to the two craft behind, and for a time all were much excited; they began to paddle as fast as they could toward the west shore, and on the way they talked earnestly and kept looking downstream. As soon as the canoes grounded, we were unceremoniously taken out of them and led behind a patch of tall sage-brush, where our guards threatened to kill us if we shouted or made any attempt to get away.

The reason for this was soon plain. A large keel-boat, with all sails set, appeared round the bend below, and came on up the river. There were four or five white men aboard, and they glanced carelessly at the two canoes that were drawn up on the shore, and at the canoemen who sat smoking near by. That they seemed to have no fear of the Indians surprised us. Evidently the great war between the whites and the Indians, of which the River People had told us, was either ended, or had not yet begun. Pitamakan thought that it had not begun, and Raven agreed with him. He said that if the war had ended, and the whites had won, this party would not have dared to take me prisoner.

If the keel-boat had passed near us, I would have struggled and shouted to attract the attention of the crew; it kept close to the farther shore, however, fully a quarter of a mile away. I cannot describe my feelings as I watched it sail out of sight above; it carried men of my own color, who no doubt would have fought for me if they had known that I was a prisoner of these wretches.

At last our captors motioned us to return to the canoes, and one of them emphasized the order by roughly pushing me. Raven shouted with anger; he rushed at the man and seized him by the throat; but three or four others loosened his hold, and held him as he raged and called upon all the Blackfeet gods for help. Pitamakan and I did all that we could to calm him, and he soon ceased to struggle. As the canoe in which they put him was moving away, he looked back and said to us:—

"I know now what she meant; it was that we should find, down on the far water, not the fish-dog skin, but death."

This new interpretation of the dream had a terribly depressing effect upon Pitamakan, and although I tried all the rest of the afternoon, I could not get him to take anything except the most hopeless view of our position.

Just before sunset we swept from the Snake into the Columbia. We had expected to see a big river, but not such an immense stream as that which spread before us; it was fully half a mile wide, and apparently very deep. At the junction the Snake itself was about a quarter of a mile wide, and for a long way down, the muddy water from it contrasted sharply with the clear blue of the Columbia.

On the south side, below the junction of the rivers, was a small fort, from which our captors kept as far away as they could. Two miles farther on, they beached the canoes near some Indian houses on the north side of the stream. All the inhabitants of the place turned out to watch us land; they were a people with flattened heads. From the base of the nose the skull sloped back to the crown at an angle of about forty-five degrees—a peculiarity that made them look deformed. The women were even uglier than the men; they were short and broad and fat, and wore no clothing except a short kirtle of twisted grass, and a miserable robe that covered their shoulders and back.

Although we could not understand a word of the talk that began as soon as the two parties met, this much was plain: our captors were of a different tribe from those of the village. Moreover, it seemed to me that the village men were not eager to become the hosts of the canoemen. Most of the men of both parties stood silent, and the two chiefs talked together; the chief of the village asked questions, and the other answered.

At last the visitor spoke a few words to his men; they closed round us, and the whole party moved forward to the village. It consisted of seven large houses built with frames of forked posts and poles, and covered with mats of long rushes. The building into which we were led was fully sixty feet long and twenty feet wide, and was occupied by five or six families.

Along the apex of the roof from one end to the other was an open space about eighteen inches wide that served as a window, and also allowed the smoke of the fire to pass out. Round the walls were hung fish-nets and spears, bows and quivers of arrows, and a few guns. Near the fire in the centre of the place were a few pots and pans, and several packages of pounded roots. Before each of our party the women placed a small portion of this stuff and a piece of dried salmon. Their action, however, was without any show of hospitality.

I could not help contrasting our reception by these half-naked people with the welcome that the Blackfeet gave to every one who entered their lodges. To their meanest guests they offered unsparingly the best that they had—buffalo meat, pemmican, berries, even clothing and horses.

Naturally we began to talk about our terrible situation. Raven was sure that he had given a wrong interpretation to his dream, and Pitamakan agreed with him. I should have had no belief in dreams, but that night I shared their superstitions to some extent. Our medicine was wrong; no doubt we were to be taken to some remote part of the country, and tortured, or fattened for a cannibal feast.

Wood was scarce in this part of the country; there was no timber, and evidently the villagers had brought on rafts from a distance the little fuel that they had. Only two or three small pieces were put on the fire at a time, and most of the long lodge was in deep shadow. People were constantly coming in to gaze at us, and leaving when their curiosity was satisfied. We were too miserable and anxious to pay attention to them.

Consequently, I almost jumped from my seat when I heard some one at the far end of the lodge ask in good English:—

"Say, are you a white boy?"

## CHAPTER VIII

"Yes, yes!" I cried, and I stood up to see which one of the persons in the shadow had spoken.

"Is he a white man?" Pitamakan asked.

Before I could reply, a canoeman gave a vicious pull to the skirt of my capote, and I went sprawling back into my seat.

As I recovered my balance and sat up, there appeared before me a white man. He was small and bent, and had white hair; like myself, he was dressed in buckskin, and wore a fustian capote. He held out his hand, and said, "How! How!"

I shook hands with him, and he sat down beside me.

"You wear a capote!" I exclaimed. "You must be a Company man—and a prisoner, too. Tell me—do you think they are going to eat us?"

He looked at me with such evident surprise that I added, "The River People told us that some tribes down here fatten their prisoners and then eat them."

"No, they don't do that," he replied. "They make slaves

of them. But I'm no prisoner; all the tribes are friendly to us Hudson's Bay Company men."

"Pitamakan! Raven! They don't eat people!" I exclaimed, jubilantly, and I saw by my companions' faces that they were as much relieved by the news as I had been.

Then I remembered that the Hudson's Bay Company was our bitter rival for the trade of the Blackfeet, and other Indians of the Rocky Mountains and the buffalo plains; I doubted whether this man would help us to escape slavery, even if he could. However, I asked, and waited in terrible suspense for his answer.

First, he wanted to know who I was, who my companions were, and where we were going when we were captured. I told him, and the only comment he made was, "Huh! Two hundred horses for a seal! My! My! My!"

"And what would you do for me if I should get ye all out of the hands of these Yakimas?" he asked. "Would ye trap and hunt for me the endurin' winter?"

I agreed to that, and when I told Pitamakan and Raven of his offer, they assented to it.

"Well, well, we'll see what we can do," he said. "It's goin' to be hard work. They believe that you're an Indian, like your partners, or at any rate, a half-breed; and you sure do look like one."

I had not thought that any one could mistake my race; but I realized then that as I naturally had dark skin and black hair, and as I was tanned still darker by constant exposure to the sun, and dressed in Indian costume, I was an Indian so far as appearances went.

The old man began to talk to our captors; at first they listened in sullen silence, but soon they began to argue with

him, and after a time there was almost a war of words between them. Just as I began to lose hope that he could
do anything for us, the wrangling ceased, and the old man
went from one to another of them, collecting our property
and passing the articles to us as he obtained them, until
we had everything, even to the needles and sinew thread
of our sewing outfit. I cannot tell how happy I was when
I held my fine little rifle once more.

"Well, come, now, and tell your partners to follow," he
ordered.

We went out of the house, and into another one at the
western end of the village. There he told an old woman,
who we learned was his wife, to give us tea and a bit of
salmon. She broiled a large fresh one, and I thought I had
never tasted anything so good.

"No American could have done for ye what I have done
to-night," he said to me. "Ai! Ai! The Company is still powerful with these people, even if its posts have been moved
across the line."

I asked him what he meant by that, and, somewhat im-
patiently, he gave a brief history of the country. He said
that until recently the whole watershed of the Columbia
and Snake rivers had been under the control of the British,
and especially of the Hudson's Bay Company, and he told
me about the events that led up to the fixing by treaty of
the international boundary-line, whereby the British lost
forever what are now the states of Oregon and Washington.

The old man described the wars between the Americans
and the Indians from 1855 to 1858, and it was plain that
his sympathies were with the Indians. Next, he told of re-
cent discoveries of gold on the Salmon River, and deplored

the fact that the whites were rushing into that country by hundreds, and that other hundreds were beginning to farm the rich lands of the Walla Walla, the Willamette, and the lower Columbia. I symphathized with him, for I, too, had been brought up to regard the Great West as the exclusive property of the Indians and the powerful fur companies.

Lastly, he told me that the factor of Victoria, the Hudson's Bay post on Puget Sound, had sent him to visit the tribes of the Columbia to get them to bring their fur catch to that post in the spring. His mission was now fulfilled, and he would start in the morning for his own winter trapping-ground on the Cowlitz River, a stream that flows into the Columbia on the north side, about forty miles from the ocean.

We set out for there the next morning in the canoe of the old trapper, whose name was Kent. None of the Yakimas or the Sokuks of the village paid any attention to our going. The canoe was a long, slender, cedar dugout, which could carry a cargo of several tons; but except for ourselves, and for the old woman who was huddled amidships, there was nothing in it except a bundle of traps, a few packages of dried roots and fish, a meagre camp outfit and bedding. The old man gave each of us a stout paddle, and took the steering paddle himself. It was Raven's first attempt at canoeing, and he did not take kindly to the work.

On the second day we came to the Dalles, a place where for several miles the great river shoots through a narrow gorge with falls and rapids. At the head of the rapids we were surprised to see many white men encamped; some were building a steamboat, and others were on their way to the gold-diggings. Kent advised me to say nothing to any of them, lest I get into trouble. The soldiers might arrest me for being with Indians, he said.

Along this bad stretch of the river there was a wooden track road, with cars that were drawn by horses; but as Kent had no money with which to pay for transportation, we spent two days carrying our stuff to the foot of the rapids. From there a day and a half brought us to the Cascades, where the great river has cut a cañon through the mountains. In several places along the way we saw dead forest trees deep down in the water; some of them were standing. Kent said that the Indians had a tradition that a great rock bridge across the river had fallen and had thus raised the water and buried the forests that lined the shores.

Here we had another portage, the last one on the river. There were many whites at this place also; as we pushed on past them as quietly as we could, the coarse remarks that they made about the Indians were almost more than I could bear. I prayed that the heartless crowd might never overrun our own Northwestern plains.

At the Cascades we left the dry and barren plains and entered a country of heavy forests. For the first time we saw Mount Hood, a tremendous dark cone, snow-crowned, and so high that even Raven gaped at it in astonishment. We had seen nothing in the Rockies to equal it. About an hour after we reëmbarked, a storm came up, and we were soon wet to the skin.

There were many islands in that part of the river, and as we threaded our way among them in the rain and the dense fog, there rose on our right a strange, muffled baying that at once reminded me of a pack of foxhounds I had once heard back in Missouri. I called the old trapper's attention to the noise, and asked him who owned the dogs.

"God owns 'em," he replied, with a grin, "and the game they hunt lives in the water. Boy, those are seals."

"Listen!" I cried to my partners. "Do you hear that barking? The old man says that the animals that are doing it are fish-dogs."

Upon hearing that, Raven and Pitamakan dropped their paddles and snatched up their guns, and peered anxiously into the fog. At first Kent laughed at our excitement; but after a moment he said:—

"Well, if I could get two hundred horses for a skin of one of them seals, I expect I'd have the fidgets, too."

He told me—and I interpreted for the others—that seals were plentiful from this place to the sea, but that it would be almost impossible for us to get one with the rifle, as seals sank as soon as they were shot. He added that he did not wish us to waste time hunting them. In the spring, when we were ready to start homeward, he would spear one for us, or would get a Chinook Indian to do it.

That was fair enough, and laying down our weapons, we began to paddle with a vim. We were actually in the country of the fish-dogs, and had heard them bark! Pitamakan started the song of the wolf, and we joined in it. Soon the old man was beating time with his paddle against the side of the canoe. "Ai, ai! Ai, ai!" he shouted, when he had finished. "That's the finest song, white or red, that I ever heard. Say, what's the name of it? Teach it to me."

Raven, who had been silent and melancholy since the evening of our capture by the Yakimas, took some interest in what was going on. "It may be just the other way," he said, later in the day. "Yes, I now believe that she meant to say we should find here that which we seek."

"Of course she did," Pitamakan declared. "Here are the fish-dogs; and here are we. Yes, brothers, I am sure that we shall succeed in our quest."

The old trapper wanted to know what our talk was about, and I told him. He listened with interest, and interpreted the story to the woman.

At last, after they had talked together for some time, he said to me, "It is often hard to understand dreams, but in his case it seems easy. You tell Raven that my old woman and I say his medicine is good. His shadow woman meant to say that you would come out all right on this thing. And here's the proof: look back at all you have been through; fights along the trail; captured by Yakimas; and here you be safe and sound, a good winter ahead, and a fair trail home in the spring with your medicine-skin. You tell them that. And let's have that wolf-song again."

Toward evening the wind changed, the fog lifted, and we found ourselves close to some large, odd-looking houses on the north shore. On the beach several canoes were drawn up, some of which were large enough to carry fifty or sixty paddlers and a heavy load of freight. We landed beside one that both at the bow and the stern had carved figureheads five feet high. One of them represented a man with three heads,—a bear's head, a frog's head, and a bird's head,—and was so horrible that both Pitamakan and Raven, muttering prayers, shrank away, and turned their backs on it.

Kent told me that the village was inhabited by Chinook Indians. Some of the people came out to meet us, and invited us to spend the night in one of the houses. These houses were different from any that we had seen. They were about fifty feet long and thirty feet wide, and were let down about six feet in the ground. The walls were of split boards, and so was the gable room, which was supported by huge posts and rafters. The wide beds of the different families were four or five feet from the floor, and were reached by ladders. Under the beds were piles of dried fish and other food. There were three fireplaces, about eight feet square, and at each of them women were roasting salmon and boiling roots. In a short time the meal was ready, and the women placed before us generous portions of the food.

Most of these people had flat heads. Several babies, who were strapped on board cradles, were having their heads flattened. Thin, smooth pieces of board were bound against their foreheads at an angle of about forty degrees, so that as they grew, their skulls were forced to conform gradually to the shape of the space between the boards.

I was curious to know the reason for this flattening, and the old trapper told me that the people thought it increased their beauty. They believed that in the very beginning of things, their god, "Dok-we-budl," ordered them to do it.

There were some men and women in the lodge who had natural heads, and I learned that they were slaves. Their children were not permitted to have their heads flattened.

Most of these slaves had been captured by the Yakimas, Cayuses, and other warlike tribes in their southern raids, and had been sold to the Chinooks. The value of a strong, healthy man or woman was about ten new, three-point blankets, or about one hundred dollars. In earlier times they had not been worth so much. When the Chinooks first obtained iron from the ships that came into the mouth of the river, they sold it to the Indian tribes at the rate of one arrow point for two slaves

Pitamakan and Raven were objects of the greatest curiosity to these villagers. In some way they had heard that the Blackfeet were a powerful and warlike tribe of the plains, and the chief asked many questions about their country and the way they lived. At last he wanted to know how many enemies Raven had killed, and would not believe that the number was nineteen until Pitamakan and I both assured him that the statement was true.

Then he said that he wished he could have Raven for a slave; I interpreted what Kent told me his words were. For a moment Raven said nothing, but his eyes were very bright and his voice trembled with anger as he replied, "Ask him if he or any of his fish-eating people ever had a Blackfoot slave?"

"One, a woman. But she drowned herself," was the reply.

"Ai! Just so," said Raven. "No Blackfoot could be a slave. We were captured the other day, and were about to be sold as slaves when this white man rescued us. I was waiting all the time to see what would happen. At the first chance I intended to get hold of a knife, or some other weapon, and kill as many of the enemy as I could before they killed me."

The talk ended there; but there was no mistaking the meaning of the looks with which the people regarded us; Raven's simple statement had instantly caused them to respect us.

We were not sorry to leave the Chinook village early the next morning. There was much about the people and their mode of life that was repulsive to us of the sunny plains. In personal appearance they were disgusting. We were accustomed to rich meat, and plenty of it, and their fish and root diet did not satisfy us. But Kent and his old wife really enjoyed their stay, and left with regret.

Not long after leaving their village, we neared a place on the north shore that Kent said was Fort Vancouver. It was once the property of the Hudson's Bay Company, but was now held by the United States. He shook his fist at it, and at the soldiers who were strolling about in front of the barracks. " 'Twas an ill day for us when we lost the place!" he muttered. And he looked so old and pitiful that I could not be angry at him for speaking of my country and its people in such a manner.

We landed in front of the big log fort, and Kent went to the trading-store to exchange half a dozen beaver hides for more beaver traps. While he was gone, three or four soldiers came and looked down at us from the top of the bank.

"Them Injuns don't look like the ones round here," one remarked.

"That's right," said another, "and just see the fine rifle that young fellow has. I'll bet he stole it somewhere. Let's call the guard and have 'em hauled up before the colonel."

If Kent had not returned just then with the traps, we might have got into serious trouble. While they were looking for the guard, we paddled away as fast as we could, and soon passed out of sight of the place round the bend. Kent said that since the big wars the soldiers were very severe with Indians who were caught out of their own country, and that I would probably have been imprisoned as a renegade white

110

boy; no matter how truthful a story I told of our harmless quest for a seal, they would not have believed me.

A short distance below the fort we passed the mouth of the Willamette River, and Kent said that there was a small town named Portland on it, not far above the junction.

All along this part of the river there were settlers. Some of them had cows and pigs—the first of these animals I had seen since I left the States. At one little farm-landing a white woman with her children stood watching us pass. I almost cried out when I saw her, because she was almost exactly like my own mother. Looking up and seeing her so unexpectedly was a shock to me.

All the rest of the day I was very low in mind. I kept seeing the pleasant little home in St. Louis; my father working in the gunshop, and whistling cheerfully as he put the finishing touches to a fine weapon; my mother singing a favorite hymn as she went about her housework. They were gone to another world; and here was I, paddling down a great, strange river, almost a thousand miles from Fort Benton, the only place I could call home.

For the first time I felt a sense of guilt in having started on this strange quest; it was true that Tsistsaki had given me permission to go, but what of my Uncle Wesley? What would he say when he returned to the fort and learned that I had left with two companions for the far western sea?

That evening we made an early camp at the entrance to a marsh that was covered with water-fowl. While we were preparing a brush shelter, Kent went out with his "scatter-gun," and soon returned with all the canvasbacks he could carry. They were very fat, and made a welcome change from the fish on which we had subsisted.

111

# THE QUEST OF THE FISH-DOG SKIN

Early the next morning, when we were eating our breakfast, Pitamakan suddenly sat up straight, dropped his duck, and, staring wild-eyed at the river, gasped, "Look! Look! See the terrible water person!"

We looked where he pointed, and saw only a widening ripple where something had sunk. Pitamakan's face was gray from fright. "It was an underwater person!"* he said.

And then, without making a ripple on the glassy surface of the river, the thing reappeared; first the snout and then the whole head of a strange animal came up close inshore. It had large, intelligent eyes, sleek, shiny fur, and was shaped not unlike an otter.

"Huh!" Kent exclaimed. "It's a seal."

"Su-yi íom-i-ta!" (Fish-dog!) I whispered to my companions, and we all reached for our guns. But as soon as we moved, the animal sank as quietly as it had appeared, and although we stood watching the river for several moments, it did not come again.

"So that was a fish-dog!" Pitamakan exclaimed. "And I thought it an underwater person! Well, brothers, we have seen the thing that we seek. I'm glad of that, but for a moment it did give me a terrible fright."

The silent Raven now spoke for the first time since we had got out of our thin bedcoverings.

"You tell the old man that I think we had better make our hunt for the water-dog now," he said to me. "Once we have the skin we have come so far to get we shall feel easy in our minds and light in our hearts, and shall be able to do better trapping for him this winter. Tell him what I say."

*The Su-yi´-tup-pi—underwater people. Fabulous inhabitants of the deeps, whom the Blackfeet greatly feared.

112

# CHAPTER IX

I interpreted what Raven said. On hearing the proposal, Kent rubbed his hands nervously together, a habit of his when in doubt, "Wait a bit," he answered, presently. "I'll find out what the old woman thinks about it."

Here was another custom of these Columbia tribes that was strange to us of the plains. The women not only had a voice in all important matters, but their work was actually shared by the men. The old couple talked together for some time, and then Kent announced that we would hunt seals before we went up the Cowlitz River. He explained that his woman wished to lay in a stock of dried clams for the winter, and that therefore we would go on down the Columbia and cross a point to Shoalwater Bay, where both seals and shellfish were plentiful.

"We shall see the ocean, then!" I exclaimed.

"Ai! That you will," he answered.

I told my partners what Kent had said, and we loaded the canoe in unusually quick time. I have always thought that the old wife's desire for dried clams carried the day in our favor.

A mile or two below the camping-place we saw the seal again, and during the day several of the animals swam within range of our guns. The temptation to shoot at them was very strong; only the old trapper's repeated assurances that they would sink at once if they were killed, prevented our firing at them.

As we went on downstream the river became wider and wider. I remember that there were many magnificent cliffs and islands along the way: and always there was the dark green forest of giant trees that stretched back from the shores as far as we could see. The general effect of the scene upon us, however, was depressing. The river was too large, too expressive of terrible power. The forests were too wide and dark and silent. And the gray clouds, the mists, and the drizzling rain that swept upstream with the west wind, chilled our bodies and numbed our spirits.

In the afternoon of that day we passed the mouth of the Cowlitz River, a large, swift stream of clear water. Some distance above it, the old trapper pointed out Coffin Rock; and about three miles below it, Mount Coffin, a lofty island on which the Indians of the vicinity buried their dead—not in trees, as the custom of the Blackfeet is, but in canoes. When a chief died, his largest war canoe was used for the burial. The body was carefully wrapped and laid in it, and then covered by a smaller canoe; his weapons, clothes, and other articles of use and adornment were placed beside the body, or hung up near it.

Kent said that at one time there had been more than three thousand of these burial canoes on Mount Coffin, and that a fire started by a certain Captain Wilkes had destroyed

114

them.

When we passed the lower place of sepulture, the old wife wept and wailed; the sight of it had called to her mind some friends of hers who were buried there. The old man told a sad tale of death and destruction along the river. When the Hudson's Bay Company first came into the country, he said, there were about thirty thousand Indians; now only a few hundred were left. Some of the tribes had become extinct. A few of the Indians had fallen in wars with the Americans; the greater number had died from pestilential diseases, and from the use of "fire-water." For all of this disaster the white men were responsible.

Late in the afternoon a stiff northwest wind kicked up a heavy sea that obliged us to turn about and make for the lee side of a point. The rise and fall of the canoe over the big waves was a new experience to us of the plains, and in a few minutes we became seasick. Almost as soon as we reached shore, we recovered, however, and as we found in the sand some fresh tracks of elk, we started into the timber in search of the animals.

Raven found a half-dozen large ones, and dropped a fine, fat bull with one shot. We hurried over to help skin it, and during the work we laughed and talked like so many children. We had come into our own again; we had meat, red, fat meat, and plenty of it.

The drizzling rain did not matter then. We built a good fire, hung over it a whole side of ribs and a shoulder, and set more choice meat strips to roast in front of the coals; as we sat under a brush shelter and watched them brown and sizzle, we were happy. The evening was passed in feasting, story-telling, and singing; and in the course of it the old trapper called again and again for Pitamakan's song of the wolf.

The next morning was calm and sunny, and we were early afloat on the great stream. At that point it was several miles wide. I could not understand the reason for the unusually swift current that bore us along, and I asked Kent about it. He told me that it was caused by the outgoing tide of the ocean; that the tide rose twice in twenty-four hours, and went out twice, and that the moon caused the tide to ebb and flow. But how it happened, Kent could not tell and during my few school-days I had been taught nothing about it. So I could explain only vaguely to Pitamakan and Raven why the shore was dry at certain times of the day and covered with water at other times.

However, they took the matter on trust, and were satisfied. Ko-ko-mik-i-is (Night-Light, the Moon) was one of the gods, and could do anything; if she chose to raise the water of the ocean twice a day, well and good. It was her affair, and none of our business.

All the morning we kept near the north shore. At noon Kent pointed out, several miles away on the south bank, a cluster of buildings that he called Fort George. The Americans, he said, had named the place Astoria. Once, his company had owned it and carried on a great trade there; but now the incoming ships passed by and went on up to Portland, and the post was falling into decay.

Soon after we had passed Astoria, we rounded Chinook Point, and entered what Kent called Baker's Bay. Here, for the first time, we had a good, although still distant, view of the ocean and of the breakers on the bar at the mouth of the river. Since a fog veiled the great distances of the

116

sea, there was nothing about the scene that was very impressive, but when I explained to my companions that it took three months to cross to the other side of it, their astonishment was unbounded.

The fog soon enveloped us, but Kent was a good pilot, and steered the canoe through it down the bay and straight into the mouth of the Wappalooche River, a small stream at the western end. Here the families of two white settlers had their homes, and there were several Indian houses. In one of these we were invited to spend the night, and in the feast that followed our arrival, most of our elk meat was consumed. Before we turned into our blankets, Kent told us that he had changed his plan for the winter trapping. Instead of returning to the Cowlitz, we would ascend a stream named the Willapa, which ran into Shoalwater Bay. It rose close to the Cowlitz, and was navigable for canoes nearly to its source.

In the morning we ascended the Wappalooche River for several miles to the portage, and then four Indians with whom we had camped started with the canoe for Shoalwater Bay, by way of the Columbia and the ocean, a dangerous undertaking if a storm should arise. I asked Kent what he was to pay them for making the trip, and he answered, "Nothing. These Indians are always glad to do anything they can for the Hudson's Bay Company. We have always treated them kindly and fairly, and that is more than you Americans have done."

I have to acknowledge that he spoke the truth.

The distance across the portage to Bear River was not more than a mile, and when we had toted our stuff over, we made a temporary camp, and waited for the Indians

117

to come with the canoe. They arrived at noon the next day, after paddling sixty miles, part of the way against a northwest wind and a heavy swell. The seamanship of the coast Indians was remarkably good, and their dugout cedar canoes were very seaworthy.

It was three miles down Bear River to Shoalwater Bay, and we dropped down quickly on a falling tide. We found a calm sheet of water about thirty miles long and from one to eight or ten miles wide; except at the entrance, it was separated from the ocean by a narrow peninsula that rose only a few feet above the water at high tide, and was covered with timber. Except, moreover, for deep channels that were cut by the rivers that emptied into it, the greater part of the bay was shallow, and at low tide vast areas of shoals were bare.

The shoals were covered with shellfish,—oysters, clams, crabs, and shrimps,—all of which were as strange to me as they were to my companions. I shall never forget the look of horror on Raven's face when, after we had made camp for the night on a small island, the old woman brought in a basketful of large and lively crabs. They were bad medicine, he said, and he refused to eat any of them, or even to touch them. Pitamakan, however, was quite willing to taste the meat of a claw when the crabs were boiled, and having tasted it, he ate as much as any of the rest of us.

We all spent the next two days gathering large clams for drying. We found plenty of them in the sand about a foot below the surface, and collected great heaps of them at the camp. There we opened the shells, strung the meat on willow skewers, and laid these on racks above a fire, to smoke the clams. Another variety, the quahaug, we laid on hot stones and covered with seaweed. When the quahaugs were cooked, the shells fell apart, and the meat was easily taken out and skewered.

There were three families of Chinook Indians near our camp engaged in the same work, and I learned that the large quantities of clams that they dried were intended for trade with tribes that lived in the vicinity of the Dalles. I did not care much for dried clams myself; they were tough, and did not have much flavor.

There were many seals in the bay, and since at low tide they gathered on bars and islands to sun themselves, I proposed to Kent that he let us go out with the canoe and try to shoot one. "You would only waste your time," he replied. "Just be patient."

That evening we visited the Chinook camp, and Kent engaged a tall, powerfully built man, about fifty years old, to spear a seal for us. Unlike other forms of hunting, this was something that could not be done offhand. The old man gravely informed us that he would first have to fast for a day and a night, and make certain prayers and sacrifices to the gods.

Two days later he came to our camp, and announced that he was ready for the hunt; he said that all the signs were right, and that he was sure we should get a seal. We all got into the canoe, and paddled across to the peninsula that divided the bay from the ocean; there we disembarked, and walked across to the outer beach. The Chinook led; he carried a spear with a fir haft about twenty feet long, on which a double barbed head was loosely set. Attached to the head was a stout line, about two hundred feet long, which hung in a coil on his left arm. We made for a small lagoon where seals were usually to be found.

Even from our camp on the island we had heard the boom of the surf of the Pacific; now, as we approached the beach through the timber, the sound was louder in our ears at every step. A sudden turn in the trail finally brought us out of the underbrush, and we faced a scene that to my unaccustomed eyes, and to those of the Blackfeet, was terrible as an exhibition of sullen power. One after another, great green waves rolled in from the limitless waste of waters, curled over, and fell upon the beach with a deafening crash and in boiling swirls of foam. I looked at my companions, and saw in their staring eyes and open mouths the astonishment that was no doubt expressed on my own face. We forgot all about the seals and Kent and the Chinook, and just stood and stared at the sight before us.

At last Kent pulled my sleeve, and shouted, "There are no seals in the lagoon! Come on, we'll go back."

I noticed then a small bay to the right of where we stood: except for some gulls on the shore, no life was visible near it. I called to my companions, and they reluctantly followed me; but several times we stopped to look back at the surf, the strangest and most impressive sight of our lives.

"And you say that it is always that way, wind or no wind?" Pitamakan asked, when we were back in the timber and his voice could be heard. "Well, I think that it must be full of the underwater people; they keep it stirred up in its terrible unrest."

"Ai! It is very terrible," said Raven. "Those who go out upon it with canoes must have strong medicine."

So they had; but it was the "medicine" of generations of experience. If those seafaring Indians had been

120

transported to the plains, put on swiftly running horses in the midst of an even more swiftly running buffalo herd, deafened by the thunder and rattle of a thousand hoofs, and choked and blinded by clouds of dust, they would have said, as we did of the sea, "Puts-ik´-stün-ah-tap-i!" (It is very terrible!")

We returned to the canoe and paddled northward for several miles. The tide was going out, and the water raced through the channels in the flats. The old Chinook stood in the bow, keeping a keen watch ahead, and with slight motions of his hands showed Kent which way to steer. We saw several seals swimming and diving in wide stretches of water, but they were not what the spearman sought. As we rounded the end of a sandy island, he suddenly crouched down, gave an order in his strange tongue, and Kent turned the canoe toward the shore.

The old Company man motioned to us to follow him, and we crept up the sand to where some rushes and grasses grew above the reach of the tide; through them we saw the quarry: three seals that lay on the point of a bar less than three hundred yards away. Two of them were apparently asleep; the other, a huge old fellow, seemed to be on guard; every few moments he would rise on his flippers as high as he could, and, sniffing the air, would look about him. Fortunately for us, the wind was from the north.

When we had left the canoe, the Chinook had slipped naked into the water. Now, when we looked back for him, he was nowhere to be seen, and the old trapper's eyes twinkled with amusement when he noticed how puzzled we were.

"Where can he be?" Pitamakan exclaimed.

"There's a seal," I whispered, and I raised my rifle to aim at a black head that bobbed in the waves close under the lee of the island.

"No, it ain't." Kent chuckled, as he pushed down the barrel of my rifle. "That's the head of our Chinook. You watch him; he's a good one."

It was interesting to watch him stalk the seals. He moved slowly; where the water was deep enough, he stood upright; where it was shallow, he crouched; never, even when he was in the very shoalest places, could we see anything of him except his head. The black top, the dark forehead and nose, and the heavy loose hair that floated behind—all combined to make his head look like that of a seal. He held the spear in his right hand under water; he had tied the end of the line round his waist, and carried the coil in his left hand.

Anxiously, we watched him approach the seals. Even Kent, who had seen the trick done many times, was excited. The Chinook moved so slowly that we thought the prey would finish their sun-bath and take to the water long before he could reach the bar. In order to deceive thoroughly the large seal that was on guard, he began, when he was halfway there, to dive and to swim under water, coming up at intervals to breathe, just as a seal does when it is fishing. Twice the guard raised up and stared at the black head, and each time the head disappeared; that evidently satisfied him that a fellow creature was coming in to doze on the sands.

Our excitement was intense. When the hunter was about twenty yards from the bar, he dived for the last time. He came up in water that was knee-deep, jumped to his feet,

122

and raising his spear, rushed toward the seals. They scrambled madly to escape, bobbing and bumping along on their flippers in the helpless way they have when they are on land. There were a few yards of sand to cross, but the man was in front of the animals; he met them in the shallow water, and for a moment there was so much splashing that we could hardly see what was going on. Soon afterward, he was out on the beach, digging his heels into the sand, gripping the line round his waist, and bracing himself to withstand the wild plunges of his victim in the water.

"Come on! He's got one!" Kent yelled; and we all ran to the canoe, and paddled as fast as we could across to the bar.

By the time we reached there, the seal was almost dead; we caught hold of the line and helped to haul it in. It was a yearling; the Chinook explained that he had speared it rather than the big male, because it would be better eating. When it had been hauled on the sand, Pitamakan, Raven, and I examined it with great interest and satisfaction. Our quest was ended; we had the skin that we had come a thousand miles to get, for which we had risked our lives and endured great hardship.

At that time we gave no thought to the risk of the return journey over the long trail. Pitamakan put our feelings into words when he exclaimed, "Puts-iksái-tam-ap-i sit-si-kös!" (What a very happy day!)

"Yes, and think of our great reward," I added. "Two hundred horses for the skin. We shall all three be well off as the result of this morning's killing."

"The reward is all for you two," Raven said. "The lone

widower has no use for more horses than he can ride. In the course of a few winters you will be setting up lodges of your own; you will need large bands."

"But some day you will set up a lodge again."

"Never," he replied sadly; "never, until I set up a shadow lodge with her in shadow-land."

"You are very generous to us," I said to him, and Pitamakan repeated my words. In Blackfoot that is the strongest expression of thanks that it is possible to use. The Blackfeet show that they are grateful more by their deeds than by their words.

Since the trapper was in a hurry to return to the work of drying clams, we loaded the animal into the canoe and paddled back to camp; we spent the rest of the day in taking off the skin of the seal and removing the fat, or blubber, from the inside of it. We gave the old Chinook fifty rounds of powder and ball for his trouble, and he went home well satisfied.

For several days after the seal-hunt we dried clams. There were many Chinooks who lived here and there about the southern end of the bay, and scattered along the northern shore were a number of families of Chihalis Indians, a tribe that comes of a different stock from that of the Chinooks, and speaks a different language. The Chinooks and Chihalis were on very friendly terms with one another; they exchanged frequent visits, and on these occasions talked in a jargon that the Hudson's Bay Company had invented.

One morning the Indians who were camped near us, as well as Kent and his old wife, were greatly excited when a messenger brought word that a whale had come ashore on the ocean side of Leadbetter Point, as the end of the long peninsula that formed the bay was called. With our weapons, and also with axe, spade, pots, and kettles, we were hurried into the canoe, and urged to paddle as hard as we could; even the old woman, with frantic energy, wielded a paddle.

It took several hours for us to reach the point. As we approached it, we saw canoes coming toward the point from all directions. In order to claim a good portion of the whale, the occupants of each canoe tried to get ahead of the rest.

We landed near the end of the point, and raced across it with a mob of flat-headed Chinooks and Chihalis. When we came out of the brush, the great whale lay before us, high on the beach, where it had been left by the retreating tide. Raven and Pitamakan and I were so surprised that we stood still. The sight of such an immense "fish," as we ignorantly called it, gave us a real shock; we could not believe that there were such immense creatures in the world.

"Stün-ah-taps!" (Fearful!) Raven exclaimed. And Pitamakan added:—

"What a wonderful story we shall have to tell our people at home."

The people were swarming upon the whale like so many flies, slashing, cutting, and gouging out large pieces of blubber with knives and axes and spades. In one place a man had already cut down so far into the body that only his head was visible as he worked. We went close to the whale to examine it, and walked round it several times. By pacing, we found that it was about seventy feet long. Kent had climbed up, and was already busily cutting blubber and throwing the chunks down to his wife; he called us to carry

125

the stuff across the point to our canoe.

At that moment, a man who was standing on the great head shouted something to the others and pointed to the northwest. The workers looked in that direction, and at once began jumping from the carcass with their tools; some of them, after picking up as much blubber as they could carry, ran toward the other side of the point. Women and children were chattering and crying, men were shouting and urging them along. We three ran round the carcass to see at what the man had pointed. Less than a mile away, a huge canoe that had a high bow and stern and that carried apparently a hundred paddlers, was coming swiftly in through the foaming breakers at the bar. Kent ran toward us, calling and wildly waving a spade. "What is it?" I asked.

"A war canoe full of Makahs!" he cried. "Come on, or you will be killed."

# CHAPTER X

Kent had told us many tales of the ferocity of the Makahs, who lived at Cape Flattery, some distance to the north, and who subsisted by hunting whales and robbing other tribes. The men, bearded, ferocious-looking fellows, were great warriors. They cut off the heads of those whom they killed, and placed them on poles set up round their homes.

"Come away! Come away!" I cried to my partners. "He says they are a war party of head-taking people."

"They shall have a chance to take my head," Raven grimly answered. "Go, you two, if you must."

His words had an immediate effect upon Pitamakan. "That is true Blackfoot talk! I shall stand beside you!" he cried.

I quickly told the trapper what they said, and his adventurous blood was also fired.

"Spoken like the brave lads they are!" he cried. "I'll make the stand with them. Wait ye here till I go get my gun from the canoe, and herd back with me these timid Chinooks and Chihalis of the bay."

127

Away he went across the point, as fast as his old legs could take him, and soon returned with more than twenty men whom he had shamed into consenting to make a fight for the whale.

Meanwhile the war canoe had come close in, heading not for the beach where we stood, but for the channel into the bay, that ran close to the end of the point. Evidently their intention was to land where we ourselves had landed, for there the water was still and deep.

The canoe was still beyond the range of our guns when the men round us began to shoot, and to dance and run this way and that way on the sand as they did so, and to shout to keep up their courage. We three and Kent held our fire until we could make it count; and we were careful not to stand together in a close group, but to keep a number of yards apart.

Nearer and nearer came the big canoe, its black and red color in sharp contrast to the blue of the sea. I counted the dark-skinned, flat-headed, shaggy-haired crew—forty-two paddlers on a side, a lookout, or pilot, standing in the bow, and a helmsman of great height and breadth, who wielded an extraordinarily long, heavy steering-paddle. The speed of the light craft, propelled by eighty-four vigorously wielded paddles, was wonderful.

When the canoe was so close that we could distinguish the coarse, broad faces, Raven cried sharply, "Now! Take aim at the man who guides!" and the reports from our three guns followed almost as one.

I cannot say that it was my ball that hit the pilot, but up he sprang, turned a half-somersault, and slid into the sea.

Immediately half a dozen of the crew pulled in their paddles, and seizing their weapons, fired a volley at us. Down fell one of the Chinooks, dead, on the sands; and another, clapping a hand to the side of his head, ran round and round in a circle, uttering shrill cries of pain. Some of the other Chinooks at the same time started to run away. Then Raven did a wonderful thing. Darting in among them, he raised the Blackfoot song of battle, and made signs to them to be brave and stand their ground; and strangers though they were to him, both in speech and customs, in some indefinable way they understood, and turning ran back with him to where the rest of us were still in line.

During the interchange of shots, the canoe had lost its headway; but now another pilot stood in the bow, and after discharging a few last harmless shots at us, the crew resumed their paddles.

"Tell the old man to order them to shoot only at the two who guide the craft," said Raven to me, and I repeated his words.

"I have already told them," Kent replied.

He had no sooner spoken than the new pilot threw up his hands and fell backward among the crew. For a moment the paddles were still; then more shots were fired at us, and another one of our number dropped upon the sand, and others again started to retreat down the point; but again Raven went after them, and brought them back. Loading and firing his rifle, shouting encouragement to us, and hurling Blackfoot defiance at the enemy, he was everywhere at once.

Again the crew plied their blades, but this time the great canoe began to circle, not toward the inner side of the point, but the other way. It was turning to go out to sea. Since it had already gone past us into the bay, and there was only the one channel, it must pass near us again on its return.

Out it came, against wind and waves, almost as swiftly as it had come in. Encouraged by the defeat of their fiercest enemy, the men of the bay ran to the end of the point, and even waded into the water, in order to fire their last few shots; but the canoe was much farther out than it had been when it entered the bay, and soon it passed beyond range.

Then, still shouting and singing, we turned and looked for Raven, and did not see him. But Kent, seeing us, pointed at a still form that lay at his feet. Instantly we understood, and ran and knelt beside the body of our friend. There was an expression of peace, even of happiness, on the face of our leader and companion.

"This is what his shadow wife meant," said Pitamakan; "that he would find death here."

With that, he began the indescribably sad, heart-rending wails of the Blackfeet for their dead; and in my quieter, white man's way, I also mourned.

Presently the women and the children and the old men, who had fled in the canoes to shallow water where the big canoe could not follow, returned to the point. Then there was more sorrow. The bay people had lost three men in the fight, and another was badly wounded. But there was rejoicing also; for the first time in many years they had repulsed the dreaded Makahs.

Some of the people soon fell to work removing the blubber from the whale. Those who had lost relatives prepared to take the bodies home for burial. A sad task lay before Pitamakan and me. Helped by willing hands, we laid the

130

body of our friend in the bottom of the canoe, and returned to camp. There Kent and his kind old wife gave us blankets and rush mats, and we all reëmbarked and went over to the east shore of the bay.

There, in the forks of a spreading cottonwood tree, we built a platform of poles and lashed the body securely on it. Beside the muffled form we laid the gun, the bow, the quiver, and a sack containing all the little articles that Raven had prized in life. Pitamakan would have it so. In the gathering night we went back to camp, and in silence sat before the fire. Now that Raven was gone, we realized how much he had been to us—how kind and helpful; in a way, both a brother and a father. It was many a day before we got over the shock of his death.

We broke camp soon after the last of the blubber had been secured, and paddled away for our winter trapping-ground. For three days we ascended the Willapa River, till we had pushed our way far into the Olympic Mountains, and found ourselves in a country alive with elk, deer, bears, and the smaller fur animals, such as the beaver, otter, fisher, marten, and mink. Here we made a camp of cedar shakes, and put out our line of traps.

It was a gloomy and a homesick winter. Traveling was almost impossible—a steady fight through thick underbrush and ferns higher than a man's head, always wet from the constant drizzling rains; and everywhere fallen trees barred the way—great trunks from six to ten feet in diameter that you could not climb over, but must go round.

Pitamakan suffered even more than I from our daily drenchings. The camp reeked with moisture, although no rain came through the roof, and before long we came to hate the dark forest and its awful silences. We were homesick, and our evening talks at the camp-fire were always of the far-away sunny plains.

The trapper and his old wife understood how it was with us, and did everything in their power for our comfort and cheer. We in turn performed our work faithfully. Every day we went the weary round of the traps, and brought home the fur they contained. The piles of valuable pelts grew fast. Kent sat and gloated over them by the hour, and fondled the dark, rich fur, and stretched the green skins with the utmost care.

"You boys are fine trappers, and you ha' not a lazy hair in your heads," he said one night. "I gave you no such promise, but I say now that you shall have a share of the catch."

"We do not want a single pelt," I replied. "All we ask is that we may start for the Missouri plains as soon as possible."

"But, boy, you are foolish to refuse the skins," he argued. "They will bring you in a good sum of silver."

His thinking that I valued money made me laugh. Not since I had left St. Louis, six years before, had I had so much as a ten-cent piece in my pocket, nor had I felt the need of money. The American Fur Company made no mention of money in its dealings either with its employees or with the Indians. Everything was valued at so many beaver-skins. Besides, Pitamakan and I were now rich. Our seal-skin, well cured and folded and suspended from a rafter of the shack, was worth to each of us a hundred horses. In the Blackfoot Country any one who owned as many horses as that was more than independent. For the gift of

132

one or two head a year, young men would herd the horses; for a share of the meat and hides, good hunters would be glad to ride the buffalo runners in the chase; and with buffalo-robes you could trade for anything the Company kept in stock.

On a drizzly night in March the old trapper decided that the time had come to break camp. We loaded the canoe the next morning, and dropping swiftly down the swollen river, arrived at the bay before sundown. From there Kent intended to go with the Indians to Victoria for the spring trade. The next day we parted from him, after he had engaged a Chinook Indian to take us down the bay and across to the Columbia River, and there furnish us a small canoe in which to ascend the stream.

"Be ye careful, now," he said, as we shook hands with the old couple. "Travel by night, and take no chances."

When it came Pitamakan's turn to take the old woman's hand, she cried and clung to him affectionately, and bade Kent tell him that she could not feel worse if he were her own son and going away forever.

When we stepped into the canoe and paddled away, our eyes were misty. The old couple had been good to us.

The Chinook faithfully carried out his orders from Kent. The canoe he gave us was small and light, just the thing for two persons to manage, although it seemed a very frail craft in which to brave the storms of the lower Columbia. Fortunately, Baker's Bay was calm when we reached it the next evening, and the light of a full moon, shimmering through the mists, enabled us to see the shore and to shape our course. After passing Chinook Point, we felt less terror of the river, and became more cheerful. For the first time since the death of Raven, Pitamakan raised the wolf-song.

When morning came, we hid the canoe and ourselves in dense timber on the north shore, and remained there and slept the greater part of the day. In similar fashion, we went on until we reached the foot of the Cascades, where we had to abandon not only the canoe, but everything else that we could possibly spare. Pitamakan even gave his bow and quiver to the sun, and prayed for help to reach our sunny plains in safety. We knew how dangerous was the long trail.

Since all of the Indian camps were on the north bank of the river, we took the south side, and night after night we followed it, living frugally on the dried elk meat that we had brought from the winter camp. Occasionally, when we were confident that no one could hear the report of a rifle, we shot a sage-hen or a rabbit in order to help out our slender supply of food.

Lying during the day in clumps of willow or sage, or among the dreary sand-dunes of the shore, we saw many canoe-loads of white men and of Indians pass up and down, but none of them saw us.

When we finally arrived opposite the point on the Snake River where the Yakimas had captured us, our food-supply had been exhausted for several days, and we had not dared to shoot at anything because of the Indians who were gathered at every rapid for the salmon-fishing. With great difficulty we collected enough driftwood to make a raft that would keep the guns and ammunition dry. Then, clinging to the raft with one hand, we swam beside it, and the current carried us far downstream. The night was very dark, and the river, swollen with the melting snows, was icy cold.

# THE QUEST OF THE FISH-DOG SKIN

All we could do was to keep kicking, and paddling with our free hands, and to trust that the few poorly lashed sticks would not be dashed against a rock. When, finally, the raft brought up on a sandbar that proved to be on the east shore, we were so exhausted and numb that another ten or fifteen minutes in the water must surely have killed us.

Shouldering our guns, the precious sealskin, and our one small sack of duffel, we staggered up the bank, and passed within a few yards of two lodges where some Indians were feasting on broiled salmon. The tantalizing odor of the fish added to our misery, and afterward we confessed to each other that at the moment we had not much cared whether we were discovered or not, so miserable was our condition.

But the next morning fortune smiled upon us. When daylight came, we found ourselves well up the stream of volcanic bedrock down which we had made our way months before. On a sandbar at a sharp turn in the channel rested a flock of swans, and when I fired at one of them, my rifle-ball passed through two of the great birds.

Although the risk was great, we determined to cook one at once. Pitamakan went up on the rim of the valley and kept watch, while I did the roasting over a fire of driftwood. Nothing happened to disturb us. When the meat was well cooked, I signaled to him to come down, and we had a good meal. After eating, we crept into a bunch of willows, and slept soundly until sunset.

From that point on, we took no chances of being discovered through cooking or traveling while it was light. With the first gray light of morning we always hid ourselves in the best place to be found at the time.

Above the falls of the Pointed Heart River, we walked

into a camp of the Pointed Hearts, but their dogs did not even growl. We cautiously retraced our steps; and since day was breaking, we had to hide in a thicket close by. We soon found that the thicket was near the trail from the camp to water. All day long people passed back and forth, and sometimes looked straight at the place where we lay. Whenever that happened, we held our breath and gripped our weapons with tense, nervous hands. The suspense that we endured until the sun went down was fearful.

We often discussed what we should do when we came to the country of the Pend d'Oreilles and the Flatheads. We finally decided that the duration of peace treaties between these tribes and the Blackfeet was so uncertain that we might find them enemies instead of friends. So we passed straight through.

You must not infer that we traveled during all the hours of every night from sundown to sunrise. There were times when the darkness was so intense that not even an owl could see its way through the forest; and again, heavy rains kept us hovering over a fire in the driest place to be found. But through all the privations of the long trail, we never lacked for good meat after the killing of the swans; and every night of travel brought us nearer home.

On leaving Flathead Lake, we chose the pass of Ün-ah-kis is-i-sak-ta* through which to cross the Rockies. There was not a horse track or a moccasin print upon it—a fact that relieved us of all anxiety about stumbling into a war party. That was fortunate, for night-traveling was out of the question here where the trail wound along the edge of

---

*Meaning Milk River. The stream that the early *voyageurs* named the Teton.

tremendous cliffs. We reached the summit of the range one warm summer afternoon, and far out to the east saw the great plains stretching away to the rim of the world.

"There it is! Our sunshine land!" Pitamakan exclaimed. "If only Raven could be with us this day!"

It was a long way from the summit down to the plains. We did not pass out of the mountains until the next after-noon, but upon seeing the buffalo and the antelope, and once more catching the odor of the sweet sage, we were well-nigh out of our senses with joy. Nowhere in all the world, we felt, was there such a rich and beautiful land as ours.

A mile or two out from the foothills we came upon a recently abandoned campground, and by the signs knew that the Blackfeet had remained there some time to cut lodge-poles and make new lodges. Their trail led straightaway down the valley, and we followed it with such light hearts that it seemed as if we were walking on air.

The next morning, after traveling two hours or so, we climbed to the rim of the valley for a look ahead. Out on the plain there was great commotion among the buffalo. A mile or two downstream hundreds of thin, spiral smoke columns were rising in the still air. One look was enough. On we went, and half an hour later we entered the western edge of the great camp.

"How beautiful and clean the new white lodges are!" I said.

"Ai! And how different are our tall, slender, well-dressed people from those squat, half-naked, and dirty fish-eaters of the Big River and the sea!" Pitamakan exclaimed.

We had no time for further talk. Some children had already recognized us, and were running ahead, to carry

137

the news of our return. The people came hurrying to greet us. They had no reason to ask where Raven was, for a little way back on the trail we had stopped long enough to rub some charcoal on our faces; so there were wails mingled with the shouts of joy that greeted us.

A few minutes later we were in Pitamakan's lodge, seated on the soft robe couches. His mother and the rest of the women were all talking at once, so excited that they were almost out of their senses. White Wolf, his father, tried manfully to conceal his emotion, but there was a suspicious catch in his voice when he spoke, and his hands shook so that only after many attempts did he manage to light his pipe.

I asked immediately about my Uncle Wesley and Tsistsaki, and was relieved to learn that they were well. For a long time it had been upon my mind that I should never see them again.

Pitamakan's first question was about Stone Arrow, and you may well believe that I also waited eagerly for the answer. They told us that he was alive, but suffering more than ever.

"Then go to him at once with this fish-dog skin," Pitamakan told his mother, "and tell him that I say this is the medicine that will make him well."

"Oh, no, my son, you must take it yourself," she answered. "No one except you must touch it until it is in his hands, else its power will be lost. Take it to Stone Arrow yourself."

We found the old man propped up on his couch, looking very thin and gray. He reached out eager hands for the skin, and his eyes burned with excitement.

"I have it! I have it at last!" he cried. "Go! Go, and leave me to pray alone with it. You are brave boys. This very day you shall have your two hundred horses."

We got them, too, choosing the number ourselves from the great herd, as the agreement was; and such was the sick man's faith in the potency of the medicine of the fish-dog skin that he was on his feet and with us, to watch our selections.

That very evening, lest there should be disputes later on as to the ownership, we started with our band for Fort Benton, in order to brand the horses in the big corral. White Wolf and several young friends accompanied us.

We arrived at the fort the next afternoon, and the welcome that I got from my uncle and Tsistsaki is one of the happiest memories of my life. There was not one reproach to mar it. On the other hand, their joy and pride in me were unbounded. There were tears in my uncle's eyes as he put his hand on my head and said, in a voice trembling with emotion, "God be praised! You are the worthy son of your father and mother. Bravery and persistence are the greatest things in the world, and you have them both."